HOUSE OF BONES

HOUSE OF BONES

Graham Masterton

This first world edition published 2008
in Great Britain and the USA by
SEVERN HOUSE PUBLISHERS LTD of
9–15 High Street, Sutton, Surrey, England, SM1 1DF.

British Library Cataloguing in Publication Data

Masterton, Graham
  House of bones
  1. Horror tales
  I. Title
  823.9'14[F]

ISBN-13: 978-0-7278-6668-4   (cased)

All Severn House titles are printed on acid-free paper.

Printed and bound in Great Britain by
MPG Books Ltd., Bodmin, Cornwall.

1

They sped through the south London suburbs in their unmarked Vauxhall Omega, weaving in and out between buses and trucks and any other driver who showed the slightest hesitation.

Detective Inspector Carter kept up a constant impatient commentary. "Come on, love. Hurry up, mate. For God's sake, you've got a green light – *move*." Beside him, Detective Sergeant Bynoe was engrossed in finishing off a pepperoni pizza.

"So what did they actually say?" he asked, sucking his fingers.

"Said they'd found skeletons. Scores of them."

Detective Sergeant Bynoe shook his head. "Bet it's a wind-up. Skeletons! Bet it used to be a medical school or something."

They turned off the main street and into a leafy square of large redbrick Edwardian houses. Years ago, this would have been a very prosperous and exclusive place to live, but most of the houses had been divided into flats and all of them looked neglected and run-down. Slates were missing, gates were off their hinges, and the scrubby front hedges were thick with an early harvest of ice-lolly wrappers.

Carter drew up on the south side of the square, where two yellow dumper-trucks were parked, and the remains of an imposing family house were surrounded by a plywood screen. Seven or eight demolition workers in hard hats were standing around smoking and talking to each other.

"Mr Garrett here?" asked Carter, showing his warrant card.

"Over there. Him in the white shirt."

"Mr Garrett?" Carter repeated, approaching a big, broad-shouldered man in a white short-sleeved shirt and a cricket club tie. "Detective Inspector Carter, Streatham CID. Do you want to show me what you've got here?"

"Never saw nothing like it in my life," said Mr Garrett. "I mean, we often find bird skeletons and cat skeletons. We found three babies' skeletons once, when we was knocking down a house in Clapham. Every time the mother had another one she stuffed it up the chimney. But nothing like this, never."

He led Carter and Bynoe through the door in the plywood screening. They crunched across smashed brick and broken glass. The top two storeys of the house had been demolished, but the ground floor remained almost intact, although the doors and the windows had been taken out and stacked neatly against the fence.

Carter could see right through to the back garden, where a child's swing still stood, a silent reminder that this had once been somebody's home.

They walked into the hall. Some of the floorboards had been ripped up so they had to balance on the nail-studded joists. Mr Garrett led them along to a wide entrance, where double doors had once hung, and into a large dusty living-room.

On the far side of the room stood a black metal fireplace. The wall next to it had been broken into, leaving a dark, gaping hole, still surrounded by brown flowery wallpaper. "Normally, like, we'd just smash the whole place down with a wrecking ball," said Mr Garrett. "But I had a couple of men in here to take out the fireplace. They're worth a few bob these days. Strip off that black paint and there's your genuine arts-and-crafts steel fireplace under there."

Carter approached the hole. He peered into it, but it was far too dark for him to be able to see anything. What struck him, though, was the *smell*. Apart from the usual demolition smell of broken brick and crumbled concrete, there was a strange aroma that reminded him of the sachets of pot-pourri that his grandmother used to keep in her wardrobe. For a moment it brought back a sensation that he couldn't quite define – a feeling of something very old, and forgotten.

"Here," said Mr Garrett, and handed him a wire-caged inspection lamp on a long lead. Carter held it up and took another look into the hole. Bynoe came up and stood close behind him and said, "Hell's teeth, guv."

Inside the hole was a large cavity between the living-room wall and the outside wall, at least four metres square. It was heaped with human bones – hundreds of them: ribcages, shoulder blades, pelvises, thighbones and skulls. Some of them were brownish and ossified. Others were so fresh and white that they gleamed. As Carter lowered the inspection lamp, a skull cast a huge distorted shadow on the brickwork, almost as if it were alive.

Carter had seen his fair share of dead bodies – people killed in car accidents, people stabbed and plastered in blood, people hanging from trees – but there was something about this huge clutter of bones that filled him with a kind of dread that he had never felt before. It was like the remains of a war.

"How many do you think?" he asked Bynoe.

"I don't know, guv. Hard to tell until we get them

out and forensics match up all those heads, bodies and legs. Twenty, maybe. Thirty. Maybe even more."

Carter took another look inside the hole. "There wasn't any kind of serving hatch here, was there?" He peered upward. "No trapdoor from the room above?"

"No," said Mr Garrett. "The whole cavity was completely sealed off."

"And none of this brickwork is fresh?"

"Well, no. You can see for yourself. It's so old that some of it needs repointing. And this wallpaper must go back to the war."

"Right," said Carter. "It looks like the whole works. Mobile incident room, scene-of-crime officers, photographers. I'd better call Barnett and tell him that we've got Armageddon on our hands here."

They worked late into the night, using arc lamps to illuminate the living-room as they opened up the wall brick by brick. Carter sat on a backless chair that he had found in the kitchen and drank scalding, tasteless coffee. Bynoe had gone to find out who had occupied the house before it was bought by the council, and who had occupied it before *them*, right the way back to the day it was first built.

Six officers carried the bones carefully out of the

cavity and stuck numbered labels on them, so that the forensic pathologists would be able to reconstruct the way that Mr Garrett's men had discovered them.

Dr George Bott stepped out of the cavity in his white protective overalls and his green wellington boots. He was carrying one of the skulls in his hand.

"Look at this," he told Carter. "This has got to be seventy or eighty years old if it's a day. The dental work is late Victorian. But there are other skulls in there which can't be more than five or six months old. How did they get *in* there?"

"It's the great Norbury bricked-up room mystery," said Carter, draining his coffee. "They'll probably still be talking about it when *we're* in the boneyard."

He stood up, and looked at his watch. "I'll come back in the morning, and see how you're getting along. There isn't very much I can do here, not till you've finished."

He was about to leave when PC Green came across the room carrying a brick. "Guv, you ought to take a look at this."

He brought it over and put it down on the seat of the chair. It was nothing more than an ordinary housebrick, except that out of one side of it a human shin-bone protruded – and on the opposite side there was the other end of the shin. The bone had penetrated the brick almost as if it were a crossbow bolt shot through a solid block of wood.

Dr Bott picked it up and cautiously examined it. "That's impossible," he said. "How can you drive a human bone through a brick? The bone's too brittle, the brick's too thick."

"Maybe the brick was made with the bone already in it."

"That's impossible, too. The bone would be burned when the brick was fired."

"Sir, there's another one here," said PC Wright. He brought over a brick from which the tips of four fingers stuck out, like the last desperate appeal of a man drowning in brick. Then another officer found three adjacent bricks with a skull embedded inside them.

"What does it mean, George?" Carter asked Dr Bott. "The whole place is full of clues but I can't understand any of them. I mean, who *were* all these people, and why would anybody want to brick them up in a wall?"

2

John was ten minutes late, and the morning was already uncomfortably hot. He was hurrying along Streatham High Road when three of his old schoolfriends came rollerblading towards him – Micky, Tez and Nasheem. They were wearing baseball caps and T-shirts and shorts, and they were drinking bottles of alcoholic lemonade.

Micky slewed around him in astonishment. "What's the matter with you, man? You've got a *suit* on. You look like you're going to your granny's funeral!"

"Yeah, what have you done to your hair?" said Nasheem. "And your earrings? What happened to your earrings? They were the lick."

Tez said, "I know. He's eighteen now. He's a *man*. So he thinks he has to dress like his dad."

"Listen, I'm late," John told them. "I'm going to get the sack on my first day."

"*Sack?*" said Tez, "You mean you've got a *job?* You must be out of your mind, man! What did you want to go and get a job for, when you could have spent the whole summer hanging out with your mates? You're not for real, you're not."

"I can't afford to hang out, not unless I work. Anyway, I've finished school now. I want to get on with making a career."

"A *career?*" gibed Micky. "What as? A bank manager? You said you were going to be the greatest rock singer that ever lived."

"I will be, when I can get a band together. But I sent off my demo and nobody wanted to know, did they? I need a really good band. I need more practice."

"So what are you going to do in the meantime?" Tez asked him. "Work for the Inland Revenue?"

"I've got to go," John insisted. "They said nine o'clock. Nine o'clock right on the dot."

"Oh, yeah?" said Micky, circling around and around him on his blades. "And *who* said nine o'clock?"

"The people I work for, OK?"

"Oh, yeah? And who are they? Conservative Central Office?"

John pushed Micky and Micky fell off his blades on to the pavement. "What are you giving me a hard time for?" he wanted to know. "What have *you* got going for you? Nothing! You're going to spend the whole summer messing around and then what? Go on the dole? I mean, what a waste of time! Even if I can't be a rock singer I'm still going to make myself some money. I'm still going to get myself some work experience."

"Go on, then," Tez challenged him. "If you're so proud of this career of yours, tell us what it is."

John hesitated, and then said, "OK. I'm working for Blight, Simpson & Vane."

"Huh? Who are they when they're at home?"

"Estate agents, OK? The best in Streatham."

Tez stared at him with his mouth open. "Estate agents? You must be joking! *Estate agents!* You're going to work for an estate agents? What a career, man! What a career! That's even worse than being a bank manager!"

John swept his hand through his hair and carried on walking. Micky and Tez and Nasheem kept following him, teasing him and gibing, but he wouldn't talk to them. He didn't want to be an estate agent. He didn't want to be anything but the greatest rock singer that the world had ever known, filling up Wembley Stadium, filling up the Rose Bowl and Madison Square Garden, singing his songs and playing his guitar. The roar of the crowd! But just before Christmas his mother had suffered a stroke which had partially paralyzed her left side;

and his younger sister Ruth was still taking her GCSEs; and his father was working extra hours on the taxi-rank just to keep the family together.

He had dreamed that his demo would lead to a million-pound recording contract, but all that he had received in return were letters saying "interesting, but sorry". John was mature enough to know why they were saying sorry. He was good, but he just wasn't good enough. And in the meantime, he had to make some money.

After a while, his friends grew bored of following him, and skated away. He turned around and watched them streak away through the crowds, whooping and punching the air. He felt a pang of jealousy.

He reached the offices of Blight, Simpson & Vane. They had an old-fashioned-looking frontage, right on Streatham High Road, with oak-framed pictures in the front window. The traffic roared past so that he could hardly hear himself think. Highly desirable five-bedroomed family residence overlooking the common. Compact two-bedroomed maisonette. Garden flat with use of garage. They were all so expensive that he could never imagine being able to buy one.

He could see his own reflection in the window and he hardly recognized himself. Last week his hair had been a wild tangle of curls. Now it was neatly cropped, right around his ears. Last week he had been wearing hoops and daggers in his ears. Now all he had was holes. He was wearing a new Burton suit and a new Burton tie and he looked just like every other pale-faced office junior in the whole of Britain – just on the verge of handsomeness, just on the verge of maturity, with dark brown eyes and a strong, clearcut jawline, and one angry spot right next to his nose.

He held his air guitar in his hands and played *Susan's House* in front of the window, watching himself as his fingers ran up and down the invisible frets, pouting and moving his hips. Eat your heart out, Eels. Move over, Beck. This is John French, the greatest rock guitarist in the history of the universe.

He had almost reached the climax when he opened his eyes and saw a long, disapproving face staring at him from over the top of the oak-framed property pictures. Instantly he stopped playing air guitar and pretended that he had been stretching instead. But the front door of Blight, Simpson & Vane was instantly opened, and a thin, beaky-nosed man came out – the same thin, beaky-nosed man who had interviewed him when he first applied for the job.

"You're late," he rapped. "I didn't think that you were going to turn up at all."

"Yeah, I know. I'm sorry. It was the bus."

"Well, you'll have to make better arrangements

in future. And in *this* practice, we say 'yesss' with an 'esss', not 'yeah.' "

"Yeah, all right then. I mean, yesss, all right then, yesss."

"You'd better come in and start work, don't you think?"

"Yesss, I think I'd better. Yesss."

"You don't have to hiss at me, for goodness' sake."

"Oh, sorry."

The man led him into the main office. It was painted pea-green, with five desks arranged diagonally down either side. The lighting was flat and fluorescent and made everybody look as if they'd been up all night. At the back of the room were rows of grey steel filing cabinets and a large-scale map of south London.

"Right, then, you probably remember that my name's David Cleat but here in the office you'll call me Mr Cleat. I'm the deputy manager."

Mr Cleat took him to the first desk, where a solidly-built, red-haired boy in a bright green shirt was eating an apple and reading *The Racing Post*. He had eyes as green as crushed bottle-glass and a splash of freckles over his nose. "This is Liam O'Bryan. Liam, I'd like you to meet John."

"Well now, welcome to the wonderful world of estate agency," said Liam, shaking his hand very hard. "You, too, can take one-and-a-half percent of everybody's hard-earned money without lifting a finger."

"Liam has a slightly irreverent attitude to what we do," said Mr Cleat, pursing his lips. "Though he manages to sell rather a lot of houses. It's the blarney. The Irish gift of the gab."

"Oh, come on now, Mr Cleat," said Liam. "Isn't estate agency all blarney? Calling a house semi-detached when it's semi-stuck-together-to-another one."

Mr Cleat ushered John to the next desk, where a young black boy was sitting, poring over a list of house prices. In front of him was a perspex name-block that announced him as Courtney Tulloch. He was so smart that he was almost unreal. He wore a navy-blue designer jacket and a red silk tie, and his hair was cropped so that the top of it was absolutely flat. He looked up and gave John a broad, unaffected smile.

"Don't take any notice of Liam," he said, shaking John's hand. "If you play your cards right, you can make a fortune in estate agency. You want a BMW? With alloy wheels? And a Kenwood sound system? You're in the right job."

"Let's think about service and integrity, as well as profit," said Mr Cleat, sniffily.

"But don't let's forget about getting ourselves a great set of wheels," Courtney grinned at him.

Mr Cleat took him along to the last occupied

desk, where a brunette girl in a yellow linen jacket was sitting in front of a word-processor, typing out the details of a desirable two-bedroomed maisonette within easy reach of shops.

"Lucy Mears," said Mr Cleat. "Lucy, I'd like you to welcome our newest recruit."

"Hi," said Lucy, giving John nothing more than a quick sideways glance. "Hope you're good at making coffee. Mine's black, one Hermesetas."

"Right then," said Mr Cleat. "I'll leave you in Courtney's capable hands. That door to the left leads to the kitchen, where you can make tea and coffee, and also to the smallest room. The staff make weekly contributions towards refreshments, and also towards, well, *tissue*."

John stared at him, uncomprehending. Mr Cleat flushed, and contorted his face into an extraordinary expression of embarrassment, pushing his upper teeth out like Bugs Bunny. "He means bog paper," said Liam, without looking up from *The Racing Post*.

Mr Cleat said, "Thank you, Liam," in a voice like concentrated nitric acid. Then he said, "That door, to the right, leads to Mr Vane's office. Mr Vane is semi-retired now, but occasionally he comes in to deal with certain favoured clients. I must advise you that Mr Vane expects a high standard of decorum."

Again, John blinked. Liam said, "He doesn't want you eating fish and chips in the office or mooning at clients who annoy you."

Mr Cleat said nothing to that, but he gave Liam a stare that would have killed a tortoise. Then he looked at his watch and said, "Anyway, I have to go. I'm meeting some prospective buyers for the Wavertree Estate, and I'm running late. I have to tell you, John, that punctuality is absolutely *essential* in this business. You must never leave people hanging about. You understand that?"

"Yeah. I mean, yesss."

As soon as Mr Cleat had left, everybody relaxed, except for Courtney, who picked up the phone and started talking to a prospective buyer about a house overlooking Tooting Bec Common. "I know you think it's too expensive, but think of the view. Grass, trees, tennis courts. If you look out of your kitchen window, you could be living on your own private estate."

"I don't know where he gets the nerve," smiled Liam. "Have you seen Tooting Bec Common on a weekend? Crowded? It looks like a tinful of maggots."

When he had finished on the phone, Courtney came over and said, "Right, John. You won't have too much to do today except make the tea and answer the phone and take the post to the post office. But I'll take you out with me when I visit some houses that people want to sell.

"There may be a couple of times when you're alone in the office, all right? If people come in and ask about any of our houses or flats, all you have to do is go to these filing cabinets, find the right particulars, and give them a copy."

He opened up one of the filing cabinets and took out a glossy folder with a colour photograph of a large six-bedroomed house on the front. "If they say they want to see it, take their name and their phone number and say that we'll arrange a visit to suit them. That's all you have to do."

"Do you always have to go with people when they look at houses?" asked John.

"Well, mostly we do, except if we're really busy, or the owners prefer to show people around themselves. Or sometimes, if a house is empty, we lend people the key so that they can go and look on their own." He opened a drawer in one of the filing cabinets. "All the keys are in here. And the alarm codes, too."

"All right," John nodded.

"There's one more thing you need to know about—" Courtney began, but at that moment his phone rang and he went to answer it. John hung around his desk, not knowing what to do, but in the end Courtney put his hand over the receiver and said, "This is going to take a bit of time. Why don't you take that desk and go through the property lists – get to know what we've got on our books."

John sat down and tried to smile at Lucy, but Lucy looked through him as if he were the invisible office junior.

3

John's first day at work was a mixture of boredom and confusion, seasoned with occasional moments of embarrassment. He spent over an hour photocopying the particulars of a block of new flats in Gipsy Hill. Then he made tea and coffee for everybody: tea with three sugars for Courtney; white coffee for Liam; black coffee for Lucy. All Lucy said was, "Where's the biscuits?" and sent him down the road to Sainsbury's for a packet of chocolate digestives. He saw two boys he knew outside Our Price records, laughing and smoking and chatting up girls. He felt trapped and frustrated, and he walked back to the office by the longest route possible: all the way along Pendennis Road and then left down Gracefield Gardens. It was hot and he loosened his tie, and by the time he opened the biscuits they had all melted. Lucy said, "Where did you go to get those? Zimbabwe?"

Just before lunch, Courtney took him out in his metallic blue BMW to meet a couple who wanted to view a small two-bedroomed house in Streatham Park. John enjoyed the drive and the car had a fantastic sound-system. Courtney turned the volume up to "deafening" and John was sure the outside of the car must be bulging out with every beat.

The house in Streatham Park was cramped and chilly and had obviously been unoccupied for a long time. There was a large brown stain on the shagpile carpet in the living-room. Somebody had stuck a poster of Barry Manilow on the back of the larder door and circled his eyes with felt-tip spectacles. The couple who came to view it were fiftyish and vague. He wore a brown nylon short-sleeved shirt and she wore a dress like a chintz chair-cover. They peered morosely into every room and made no comment whatsoever, except at the end, when the husband said, "What's the soil like round here? Acid or alkaline?"

"Clay," said Courtney.

"Well, that's no good, then. I want to grow azaleas."

On the way back to the office, Courtney said, "You want to do them an injury sometimes. I mean, you physically want to beat them up."

He laughed, and John laughed, too. He was beginning to think that he might grow to like this job, after all.

At lunchtime, Courtney invited him to come along to McDonald's for a cheeseburger and fries, but he said no.

"Listen, man, I'll pay for you. I know what it's like when you first start work."

"No, no. I've got enough money. I'm just not hungry, that's all."

"All right, then. Please yourself."

Lucy said, "Well, if you're going to stay here, I'm going to go and do some shopping."

They closed the door behind them and left him alone. The truth was that he was starving, but he only had enough money for his bus fare home, and he was too embarrassed to admit it. His dad had offered him lunch money but he hadn't wanted to take it.

Mr Cleat had given him a desk right at the front of the office, so that he would have to get up and greet anybody who wandered in. He had a PC terminal which he didn't know how to use, a blotter, and a pencil holder with Blight, Simpson & Vane printed on it.

He opened all the drawers but they were empty except for a few stray paperclips and a scenic postcard from Rhyl: *Dear All, it hasn't stopped raining since I got here. Love, Bill.*

Time seemed to crawl. John leafed through the local *Property Gazette*. Then he went to the window and stared out over the oak-framed display board, in the same way that Mr Cleat had stared at him. Streatham High Road was dusty and bright, and he saw lots of girls in very short skirts. His stomach made a noise like a cistern emptying.

He made himself a cup of coffee and ate three chocolate digestives all stuck together like a sandwich. He was wondering if he ought to risk eating another chocolate digestive when the front doorbell jangled, and a tall man in a cream-coloured blazer walked in. He had a big, suntanned face, immense eyebrows and thick horn-rimmed glasses. He banged down a brown leather briefcase on to John's desk and said, "66 Mountjoy Avenue!" His voice was so booming that John could have heard him three miles away.

"Oh," said John.

The man stared at him for a very long time without saying anything. Then, enunciating his words as if he were speaking to a complete idiot, he said, "I want to look at it."

"Oh," said John.

"I called last week. I spoke to David about it."

"Oh, I see, Mr Cleat. He's not here at the moment. Nobody's here at the moment."

"*You're* here at the moment."

"Yes, but this is my first day."

"What difference does that make? All I want is to look at it. I've been trying to find a house in the Mountjoy Avenue area for God knows how long. They only seem to come on the market when somebody dies."

"Well, I'm sorry. There's nobody here at the moment."

"I can borrow the key, can't I? I can have it back to you in three-quarters of an hour."

"I don't know. I—"

"Listen, sonny, I've been using this estate agents since you were in nappies. David and I play golf together. The house is empty; there's nothing to steal. And I don't exactly look like a squatter, do I? Or do I?"

"No. Well, no."

John went to the drawer and sorted through the keys. They were all in alphabetical order and all clearly tagged, but there was no sign of a key for 66 Mountjoy Avenue. "Sorry," he said. "It isn't here. If you could come back later..."

"I can't come back later. I've got an important appointment at two. You must have a key. David said that it was one of your special properties and that Mr Vane was dealing with it."

John shrugged. "I'm sorry. If the key's not in here—"

"Well, perhaps Mr Vane's got it in his office, if it's one of his properties."

"All right," said John, unhappily. "I'll have a look."

He cautiously opened the door to Mr Vane's office and stepped inside. The blinds were drawn so that the office was very gloomy. There were rows of old mahogany filing cabinets and a huge mahogany partner's desk heaped with papers and books. On the wall was a portrait of a good-looking woman in a crimson 1920s dress.

"Come on, lad, I haven't got all day," the man urged him.

John opened the middle drawer of Mr Vane's desk. It was crammed with an untidy collection of spectacles, pens, elastic bands, envelopes and old photographs. In the left-hand drawer there were bundles of letters tied with pink tape. In the right-hand drawer he found the keys – nine of them in all, and each of them clearly tagged. Here it was – 66 Mountjoy Avenue.

"Have you found it yet?" the man demanded.

John hesitated. Surely it wouldn't do any harm to let somebody *look* at one of Mr Vane's properties? If he liked it, he might make an offer, and surely Mr Vane would be pleased about that, even if he hadn't been here at the time.

He closed the drawer and returned to the main office.

"Well done," said the man, and held out his hand. He had a thick wedding ring, made of intertwined bands of yellow and white gold, like a rope.

John closed his fist around the keys. "I think I'd better write down your name. You know, it's my first day and I don't want to get into trouble."

"Rogers," said the man, impatiently.

John wrote it on the Blight, Simpson & Vane notepad. "And address?" he asked.

"David knows where I live. He's been to dinner, for goodness' sake."

John kept his pen poised over his pad.

"All right, then," the man told him. "103 Welham Road."

John slowly wrote down the address while the man tutted and fidgeted. When John handed him the key he marched out of the office, almost colliding with Courtney as he came back in.

"Who was *that*?" Courtney wanted to know.

John held up the pad. "Mr Rogers. He wanted to look at a house, so I lent him the key. I hope that's all right. I made sure I got his address."

"That's great. If he buys it, you'll get some commission. At this rate, you'll have your BMW by Christmas."

"Thanks," said John, and felt extremely pleased with himself. "Do you want a cup of coffee? I was just going to make one."

"Yes, great," Courtney said. "What you can do this afternoon is sort out some of these files. Any property that's been on the market for longer than three months put over here, so that we can discuss whether we're going to re-advertise it in the property papers, and whether we're going to advise the owner to cut his price."

"All right. I see."

At that moment, Lucy and Liam came back. Liam was telling Lucy a long shaggy-dog story about Tarzan applying for a job-seeker's allowance because there was no work in the jungle.

"How was your lunch hour, John?" said Liam. "Sell any property while we were out?"

"He may have done," said Courtney. "Somebody came in asking to look at a house."

"That's terrific. I hope it was The Cedars. We've been trying to get rid of that mouldering old heap for nearly three years now."

"No. It was 66 Mountjoy Avenue."

Liam stared at him with his mouth open. Courtney covered his face with his hands. Lucy said, "I don't *believe* it!"

"What?" said John. "I didn't do anything wrong, did I? The man said he knew Mr Cleat. He said he played golf with him and had him to dinner and everything." He could feel his face reddening and his heart starting to thump.

Lucy said, "66 Mountjoy Avenue is one of Mr Vane's properties. It's on his special list. He doesn't allow anybody else to sell houses on his special list."

"Where did you get the keys?" asked Liam.

"I looked in Mr Vane's desk."

"He looked in Mr Vane's *desssk*!" said Courtney, through clenched teeth. "He's going to go *ballistic*!"

"I didn't know," said John. He was close to tears. He kept swallowing and swallowing to clear the catch in his throat.

"Didn't you tell him?" Lucy asked Courtney. "Oh God, Courtney, you should have told him!"

Courtney looked at his Rolex. "How long ago did he leave? Maybe I could catch him before he gets there."

"About ten minutes ago," John told him.

What did it matter if he had given the key to Mr Rogers? He hadn't actually tried to sell him the house or anything like that. He wouldn't have known how.

Liam put an arm around his shoulder and said, "It's all right, John. It wasn't your fault. You weren't to know, were you? And you thought you were doing the right thing." John nodded: he didn't trust himself to speak.

Lucy said, "All we can do is wait for Mr Rogers to bring back the key and hope that he isn't interested in making an offer."

They were still talking about 66 Mountjoy Avenue when Mr Cleat came back, carrying his brown leather briefcase and a Tesco's shopping bag containing a bottle of Lambrusco, a chocolate eclair and a frozen lasagne dinner-for-one. "What's going on?" he demanded. "This is supposed to be a working estate agency, not a mother's meeting."

Liam kept his arm around John's shoulder. John appreciated his protectiveness but really wished that he wouldn't. It made him feel ridiculously young and stupid.

"John here's made a bit of a boo-boo," said Liam. "A fellow came in and he gave him the keys to 66 Mountjoy Avenue."

Mr Cleat put down his bags and blinked at John as if he didn't know who he was or where he had come from. "You did *what?*" he said.

"His name was Rogers," said John. "He told me he knew you."

"He does. He does know me. But you gave him the key to 66 Mountjoy Avenue?"

"It wasn't John's fault," said Courtney. "I forgot to tell him about Mr Vane's special list."

Mr Cleat opened and closed his mouth as if he were finding it difficult to breathe. He walked over to his desk and then he came back again. "What are we going to do now?" he asked. "What on earth are we going to do now?"

"I've got his name and address," John told him. "And he did promise to bring the key straight back."

Mr Cleat didn't seem to hear him. "Maybe the phone's still on. We could try calling him."

"I could go round there if you like," Courtney suggested.

"No, no," Mr Cleat insisted. "I'll go round there myself. I don't know what Mr Vane's going to say. He's had another attack of asthma this week and he isn't in the best of sorts, believe me."

John said, "I'm sorry. I'm really sorry. I didn't know."

Mr Cleat handed his Tesco bag to John and said, "Put this in the freezer compartment, will you? If anybody wants me, I'm out, and my mobile's out of order, too."

With that, he hurried out of the office. John could see him running across to the car park on the other side of the High Road, dodging in between buses and lorries.

"I don't get this," he said. "It's only a house. What difference does it make *who* sells it?"

"I don't get it, either," said Lucy. "But if there's one thing you learn when you work for Blight, Simpson & Vane, it's 'do what you're told and don't ask stupid questions.' "

"Oh," said John. "I'm sorry. Do you want a cup of coffee?"

"Go on, then," Lucy told him, and for the first time that day she smiled at him.

Mr Cleat came back over an hour later. He walked straight back into Mr Vane's office and dropped the keys to 66 Mountjoy Avenue back into the drawer. He looked pale and upset, as if he'd witnessed a road accident.

He came up to John and said, "We never, *ever*, release the keys to any of Mr Vane's properties. Do you understand me? Never! I'm willing to accept that this is your first day, and that Courtney failed to warn you about the special list. But if anybody makes an enquiry about any of our properties, you always check in the file first. If it's on Mr Vane's special list, then you take the interested party's name and particulars, and you leave a note on Mr Vane's desk for his attention. That's all you have to do."

John nodded. "I've got it now. I'm sorry. I wouldn't have done it if I'd known."

"Yes, well. Let's hope that Mr Vane is as forgiving as I am."

John spent the rest of the afternoon pasting colour photographs of houses on to display cards, and answering the telephone. But every now and then he glanced over at Mr Cleat and wondered why he had got into such a blind panic about 66 Mountjoy Avenue. And why did Mr Vane insist on keeping a special selection of properties all for himself? John thought that he would be really pleased if one of his staff sold a house for him, not angry.

He was still thinking about it at the end of the day when Mr Cleat suddenly snapped his folder shut and said, "That's it. Five-thirty. I think we've all had enough for one day."

4

He arrived home at six and his father was already grilling pork chops for supper. His mother was sitting at the kitchen table in her dressing-gown, with a cup of tea. Her hair had turned white since her stroke, and she looked much older than she really was. But at least she could talk and use her right hand, and she was able to shuffle around the house.

His father had aged, too, although maybe John was just growing up and seeing him clearly for the first time. John was now three or four inches taller than he was, and he had an aerial view of the bald spot on the top of his father's head, the size of a fifty-pence piece.

"Well, then, how's the property tycoon?" said his father.

John bent over and gave his mother a kiss. She reached up and touched his cheek and smiled her slanting little smile. "What time's Ruth coming back?" John asked.

"Oh, late. She's going out with that Peter Mills again. She can cook her own supper."

His father turned the chops over with a fork and put the broccoli on to boil. "But how was your day? Did you like it?"

"Oh, it wasn't bad. I didn't do much. Bit of filing, that's all."

"Didn't sell any million-pound houses, then?"

John thought about Mr Rogers, and the key that he shouldn't have given him, and shook his head.

"But you think you're going to like it?"

"I don't know. I suppose so."

His father said, "That's the trouble with you. You drift through life not knowing what you want. No ambition, that's your problem. No targets. Your sister's the same. She's going to end up married to some stupid no-hoper like Peter Mills, with three kiddies hanging round her ankles before she's twenty-one, and a two-bedroomed council flat in East Croydon."

"Come on, Reg," chided his mother, out of the side of her mouth. "It's only his first day."

They sat around the kitchen table and ate their supper. John's father had to cut his mother's supper up into small pieces, like a child's meal, so that she could eat it all with a spoon. Afterwards, John washed up the dishes and put them away. His mother and father were sitting on the sofa watching *Coronation Street*. "I'm just going out for a bit," he told them.

"Not too late," his father warned him. "Don't forget you've got work tomorrow."

How could I possibly forget? he thought, as he stood in front of his bedroom mirror combing his hair. *I've had just about the worst day in my entire life and it's probably going to be even worse tomorrow.* He opened his wardrobe door. Inside were dozens of pinups of girls and rock stars and Crystal Palace football team. He picked out a black Yves St Laurent sweatshirt which his father had bought for £12 from another cabbie. It was probably a fake but it was his favourite. He splashed himself with aftershave and left the house by the back door.

Down by the parade of shops he met four or five of his friends. They were larking around outside the local corner shop, smoking and teasing some girls. He joined in, and for the next two hours he forgot all about Blight, Simpson & Vane, and Mr Rogers, and 66 Mountjoy Avenue.

The next day he made himself some sandwiches before he left home, and he made sure that he arrived at work at five minutes to nine. Mr Cleat was already there, sorting through a heap of contracts. "Good morning," he said, coldly, as if it were just as much of a sin to turn up five minutes early as it was to turn up five minutes late.

"Oh. Good morning, Mr Cleat. Another hot one, eh?"

"Another hot what?"

"Well, you know. Day?"

Mr Cleat sniffed. "Make me a cup of tea, would you. And I wouldn't mind a touch more sugar than yesterday. I'm not a diabetic."

John went to put on the kettle. As he was waiting for it to boil, Liam arrived. John heard him say, "Good morning, Mr Cleat. Another hot one, eh?"

Mr Cleat said nothing. Liam waited for a moment, and then said, "Please yourself."

It was an unexpectedly busy morning. Three couples came in to look at particulars for The Old School House in Tooting Bec, and then a fussy man wanted details on every house in the Valley Road area which could easily be converted into bed-sitting rooms. John had to go to the photography shop twice to pick up developed pictures of new properties, and to the delicatessen once to get Lucy a cream-cheese and cucumber sandwich and a bottle of Perrier water.

The office was crowded when the door suddenly opened and – for a long, dramatic moment – stayed open. Everybody turned their head. Standing in the doorway, half-silhouetted against the bright

34

sunshine outside, was a tall, almost skeletal man in a Panama hat and a grey double-breasted suit with a black silk handkerchief tucked in the pocket. As he stepped inside, he took off his hat, revealing a head of iron-coloured, slicked-back hair. He looked about fifty-five years old, with a thin, sharply-chiselled face and hooded, almost colourless eyes, like a hawk's.

Mr Cleat stood up immediately, as did Liam and Lucy. Courtney was visiting a house by Streatham Common. The man walked through the office, saying, "Good morning," in a crackly, phlegmy voice like somebody slowly crumpling up a crisp packet. He went straight through to the office marked *R. Vane* and closed the door behind him.

"I wasn't expecting to see *him* in today," said Liam. "He usually plays golf on Tuesdays. At least that's what he says. I can't really picture him in those checkered golfing trousers, can you?"

Mr Cleat was obviously agitated. He approached Mr Vane's door and then he went back to his desk again. Then at last he plucked up the courage to go up and knock. There was an agonizingly long pause and then the door opened just a fraction and Mr Vane beckoned Mr Cleat to come in.

"They'll be talking about the Mountjoy Avenue business," warned Liam. "But don't you worry. Cleaty may be a creep but he usually sticks up for his staff."

After five or ten minutes, Mr Vane's door opened again and Mr Cleat came out. "John, Mr Vane wants a word."

John glanced worriedly at Liam. Liam gave him a grin and a thumbs-up, but he still couldn't stop himself from swallowing and swallowing, and the palms of his hands tingled. He knocked on Mr Vane's door and went inside.

As before, the office was almost dark. Mr Vane was sitting at his desk, leaning back in his chair so that he was almost hidden behind the mountain of pamphlets and books and particulars.

"I gather that you made a serious error yesterday," said Mr Vane, making no attempt to introduce himself.

John said, "I'm sorry, sir. It was my first day. I didn't know," in a voice that was very much higher than he had intended.

"Well, it wasn't entirely your fault. Mr Cleat should have made it clearer to you that on no account are you to have anything whatsoever to do with my properties, and certainly on no account are you to go rifling through my desk. No *rifling*," he repeated, as if it were some kind of disgusting, unspeakable sin.

"However, considering that you are new here, and Mr Cleat says that you seem to be showing promise, I am prepared on this occasion to put the matter behind us."

"Yes, sir. Thank you, sir."

"Let me tell you, though, that you are not to concern yourself in any way with any of the properties on my special list. They are mine to deal with, and mine alone. Any further mistakes and I will immediately let you go."

"Yes, sir."

Mr Vane stood up and pushed back his chair. He walked around his desk with his hands on his hips and came up very close to John and stared into his face. He was so close that John could see every wrinkle around his mouth, and how yellow his teeth were.

He laid his hand on John's shoulder and looked steadily into his eyes. "It's a great thing to be young, isn't it?"

"Well, it depends."

"I was your age once. Just starting out in life. It seems like a very long time ago now. You mustn't squander it, you know. It will never come to you again."

"Right," said John. He wished the old so-and-so would stop clutching him so tight.

"I'll give you two words of advice," said Mr Vane. "The first is, to keep your nose out of where it's not wanted. The second is, never to make promises that you'll live to regret."

John nodded furiously as if he understood what this was all about.

"Do you understand me?" asked Mr Vane.

"Yes, absolutely."

"Then you'd better go and get on with your work."

John left Mr Vane's office and went back to his desk. Lucy prodded him with her pencil and said, "You're looking white as a sheet. Are you all right?"

"Yeah, yeah. I'm all right."

"Well, let me buy you some lunch. I know you didn't eat anything yesterday."

"It's all right. I've brought sandwiches today." He patted the bag on his desk.

Before he could stop her, Lucy had opened up the packet, peered inside, and peeled apart one of his sandwiches to see what was in it. "Raspberry jam?" she said, wrinkling her nose up. "You can't work all day on raspberry jam. I'll buy you fish and chips down at The Lighthouse."

John's cheeks turned from ashen to burning red. But when he turned around he saw Liam winking at him and mouthing the words, "Go on," and so he turned back to Lucy and said, "Yeah, thanks. That'd be great."

The fish and chips turned out to be the best fish and chips he had ever eaten in his life, and Lucy turned out to be quite different from the sour, stand-offish person she had seemed to be yesterday. She was funny, and incredibly sarcastic about everybody at Blight, Simpson & Vane; and although he hadn't thought she was very pretty yesterday, he suddenly saw her in a completely new light. She had wide blue eyes and a pouty mouth and a very mischievous laugh.

"I didn't think you liked me yesterday," he said, as he finished the last dregs of his Coke.

Lucy took out her handbag mirror and admired himself. "Do you think I need a nose job? No, I make it a rule never to like anybody on their first day. They might turn out to be total nerds and then where would you be? Friendly with a nerd."

"But you don't think *I'm* a nerd?"

"Nerd-*ish*, at times. But you'll grow out of it. Just have a bit more confidence."

As they walked back to the office John said, "That Mr Vane's weird. He gave me the creeps this morning."

"Oh, there's all kinds of rumours about Mr Vane. Liam thinks he's a vampire. Courtney breaks out into a sweat just being in the same office with him. He'll be dead glad he wasn't there today."

"What do you think?"

"*I* think that he's got a terrible, terrible secret. It's so awful that he doesn't want anybody else to find out what it is. He's got a different piece of the secret hidden in each of the houses on his special list, and that's why he won't let anybody else handle them, except him."

"And what's the secret?"

"How should I know? If I knew what it was, it wouldn't be a secret, would it?"

That night, after his mother had gone to bed and Ruth had shut herself in her bedroom to play records, John and his father sat together in the sitting-room, watching television. They didn't say very much, but they were both tired, and they didn't really have to.

After the news, John's father stood up and stretched. "Think I'll turn in now. I'm starting at six tomorrow."

He was just about to switch off the local news round-up when a face suddenly flashed on the screen. John said, "Dad – don't! I want to listen to this!"

"What?" said his father.

The newsreader was saying, "... *missing from his home in Streatham. Police say that he was due to keep an important business appointment yesterday afternoon at two o'clock but failed to turn up. His car was found in a backstreet near Streatham Common station, containing his briefcase and other business papers. So far there are no clues as to where Mr Rogers might have gone.*"

"It's Mr Rogers," said John, excitedly. "Dad – Dad, it's Mr Rogers!"

"Who's Mr Rogers when he's at home? Not the chap who used to own the pet shop?"

"No, this is another Mr Rogers. He came into the office yesterday and asked me to give him the key to 66 Mountjoy Avenue. He was the man I got into trouble for."

"You didn't tell me you got into trouble. What — on your first day?"

"No, look, listen! He wanted the key to 66 Mountjoy Avenue and I gave it to him when I shouldn't have. But Mr Cleat went out and got it off him. But now he's missing."

"Well, that's not *your* fault, is it?"

John said, "No. No, it isn't. But he's missing, isn't he? He could have been kidnapped, couldn't he? He could have been killed!"

His father stood by the door and looked mystified. "If you say so," he said.

5

As soon as Lucy arrived at the office the following morning John frantically beckoned her into the kitchen. She was wearing a black short-sleeved blouse and a short white linen skirt and she had pinned up her hair.

John said, "Did you see the news last night?"

"No, I went to a club."

"Mr Rogers was on it. The man I gave the key to 66 Mountjoy Avenue. He's gone missing."

"What are you talking about?"

"I gave him the key, right? Then Mr Cleat went after him, and brought the key back. But Mr Rogers was supposed to go to a business meeting at two o'clock, but he never showed up. They found his car by Streatham Common station, with his briefcase in it and everything. And I turned on the news this morning and he hasn't been home, either."

"So what?"

"So Mr Cleat was probably one of the last people to see him, wasn't he?"

Lucy frowned. "I suppose so. But what would Mr Cleat want to kidnap anybody for?"

"Well, I don't know. But you said yourself that Mr Vane has a terrible, terrible secret, and that every one of his houses contains a different part of it. Supposing Mr Rogers went to 66 Mountjoy Avenue and discovered part of the secret? Supposing that Mr Cleat was told to keep him quiet?"

"You've been watching too much television," said Lucy. "Now, how about a cup of coffee? That's what you're here for, isn't it?"

"If Mr Rogers isn't at 66 Mounjoy Avenue, where is he then?"

"What?" Lucy demanded, wrinkling up her nose. "You think he's still there?"

"Well, he could be, couldn't he? I mean, tied up or something. Or dead."

"What? You don't think that Cleaty could *kill* anybody, do you? He puts wasps out of the window in his handkerchief."

"But if this secret's so terrible—"

"I was making it up," said Lucy. "Mr Vane is

probably just as ordinary as you or me. Well, *me*, anyway."

"But supposing you're right? Supposing it's true? And supposing Mr Rogers went into the house and found out what it was?"

"John, you're letting your imagination run away with you."

"Well, yes, perhaps I am. But all I know is that I gave the key to Mr Rogers, and Mr Cleat went to the house to collect it from him. He *must* have met him at the house, because he didn't know where Mr Rogers was going afterwards, did he? Mr Rogers didn't turn up to his first afternoon appointment, which was two o'clock, and that was the last that anybody saw of him."

"But what about his car? That wasn't outside the house, was it?"

"Of course not. Mr Cleat drove it away and abandoned it and then he walked back to pick up his own car."

"Oh, come on, John. This is silly."

"No, it's not. I think we ought to go up to the house and have a look around."

"I can't. I've got a client at eleven."

"There's plenty of time. It's only half-past nine."

Lucy hesitated, but then she saw that John was deadly serious. He had stayed awake almost all night thinking about Mr Rogers and Mr Cleat, and the more he thought about it, the more convinced he was that Mr Cleat must have had something to do with Mr Rogers' disappearance. It was the way that he had panicked, and the way that he had come back from 66 Mountjoy Avenue looking so grim-faced. It was the way that he had danced round Mr Vane, so nervy and obsequious.

Lucy went straight to Mr Cleat and said, "Is it all right if I take John to look round The Rookery?"

Mr Cleat looked up and said, "Any particular reason?"

"Well, yes. I think he ought to see how we evaluate blocks of flats. Leasehold, service charges, all that stuff."

"All right, then. Good idea. I don't see why not."

"Thanks, Mr Cleat," said John, with a wide, artificial smile, and he could tell by the look on Mr Cleat's face that he didn't know whether to be highly pleased or deeply suspicious.

"I think this is totally mad," said Lucy, as they drove past Streatham Common in her bright red Mini Metro. "And if I'm late for my appointment I'm going to kill you."

On the common, people were cycling and rollerblading and walking dogs and flying kites.

John said, "But think about it. Nobody else could have known that Mr Rogers was visiting Mountjoy Avenue except us. Otherwise the police would have been round to see us already, wouldn't they?"

"I don't know. I still think this is insane."

They turned at last into Mountjoy Avenue. It was a long tree-lined road with huge Edwardian redbrick houses on either side, most of them concealed behind high walls or laurel bushes. A few of them had been converted into nursing homes, and one of them was a doctors' practice with a shiny brass nameplate outside, but most of them were still private. Lucy drove along to the far end of the road and stopped outside number 60.

"66 is further up," said John.

"Yes, but real detectives don't park their car right outside the suspect's house, do they?"

They climbed out and cautiously approached number 66. It had a wall topped with cast-iron spikes, and heavy black cast-iron gates, but the hinges had rusted long ago and the gates couldn't be closed. Beyond the gates was a curved shingle driveway, and a chaotic front garden filled with weeds and overgrown shrubs. Five stone steps led up to the front door, which was guarded by two stone lions, one of which wore a poisonous green cape of dried-out moss.

The house itself was enormous, with turrets and balconies and gambrel roofs. Scaffolding had been erected on one side of the house but there was no sign of any workmen. All of the windows were dark and blank. High on the slated roof, a weathervane was stuck pointing NE, where the coldest winds came from.

John and Lucy walked halfway up the drive, their footsteps crunching in the shingle. They stopped and listened. Inside the grounds of number 66 it was oddly quiet, even though there was a main road only a hundred metres away, and a children's playground at the end of the street.

"You've got the keys?" asked John, and Lucy held them up, swinging them on the end of her finger. "Let's hope that Mr Cleat doesn't notice they're gone."

"He won't. You won't catch *him* daring to go through Mr Vane's desk."

They approached the front steps, and cautiously climbed up them to the front door. The door itself was painted in blistered black, with a huge bronze knocker on it in the shape of a snarling animal's face. "That's welcoming," said Lucy.

John peered through one of the stained-glass panels in the door, one hand shielding his eyes, but all he could see was a blur of blood-red light.

"Are we going in or not?" asked Lucy. "I haven't got very much time, remember."

John nodded. "Let's do it." And Lucy slid the key into the lock, turned the handle and opened up the door. It didn't groan, like a door in a horror film. Instead, it opened in total silence, which John found even creepier.

"After you," said Lucy.

They stepped into the hallway. It was high and gloomy, with a checkered tile floor and dark oak panelling all around it. On the left-hand side stood a huge carved hall-stand, with hooks and mirrors and a place for propping umbrellas. On the right, a wide oak staircase led up to the first-floor landing. On its newel post stood a bronze statuette of a blindfolded woman holding up a torch.

"Perhaps we'd better split up," John suggested. "You take the upstairs and I'll take the downstairs."

"I'm not splitting up," said Lucy. "This place is far too spooky for me."

"All right, then. But we'd better be quick."

They walked into the living-room. It was enormous, with five huge windows overlooking the front of the house and the garden at the side. It had a cavernous marble fireplace and a chandelier that was cocooned in spiders' webs. There was a rumpled, threadbare carpet in the middle of the floor, but the only furniture was a dilapidated chaise-longue and a small card-table.

Their footsteps echoed as they crossed the room and opened the folding doors that led to the dining-room. Against the far wall stood a sideboard with a mirror behind it. John and Lucy approached it and looked at themselves. "I don't look as scared as I feel," said Lucy.

They were just about to leave the room, however,

when John caught a flicker of a shadow in the mirror behind him. He swung around, with the hairs on the back of his head fizzing with fright.

"What's the matter?" said Lucy. "John – what's the matter?"

"I think I saw somebody."

"What do you mean, you saw somebody? Don't play games!"

"I'm not! I promise you, I looked in the mirror and I saw somebody crossing the sitting-room behind us."

6

He hurried across the sitting-room and back into the hallway. He looked left, and right, and then he looked up the stairs. Lucy followed him.

"I think we'd better leave," she said. "If there's somebody here, they could be anybody. A tramp or a squatter or somebody like that. They could be violent."

"But I can't understand why I didn't hear them. They didn't make any noise at all."

"John, I think this is a really bad idea and I think it's time we went."

But John ignored her. His heart was beating fast and he was excited as well as scared. He walked to the bottom of the stairs and called out, "Hello! Can you hear me? Is anybody there? We're looking for Mr Rogers!"

His voice echoed around the house, going from room to empty room and finding no reply. He turned back to Lucy and said, "Let's try upstairs. If they've got Mr Rogers tied up anywhere, that's where he'll probably be."

"Do we have to?" she said.

"Supposing he's there, all tied up, or injured, and we just walk away and leave him because we're scared?"

John started to climb the stairs, and then Lucy reluctantly followed him. They reached the galleried landing and peered back down to the hallway floor which looked like a chessboard. John said, "I'll check all the bedrooms on this side, you take the other side."

"What shall I do if I find anything? Will a scream be all right?"

John took the west side of the house. The first door he opened was a large airing cupboard, stacked with yellowing sheets and pillowcases. The next was a bathroom, with a huge green bath. The tap must have been dripping for years because the bottom was filled with a dark, rusty stain, as if somebody had been murdered in it.

He pushed the door open a little wider and stepped inside. There was a shower cubicle behind the door, with frosted glass doors. Through the frosting he was sure that he could make out a dark, hunched shape. He looked at the washbasin and saw his reflection in the discoloured mirror on the wall. His eyes were wide and he looked extremely pale.

He approached the shower cubicle cautiously and tried to see what was inside it. It looked as if it were reddish–brown, and bent over, the size of a large child. Behind him, the tap kept up its monotonous dripping. *Plick – plack – plick – plack.*

He didn't know whether he dared to open the shower cubicle or not. Whatever was inside it, it wasn't Mr Rogers – unless it was *part* of Mr Rogers. His heart was racing so fast that it was almost tripping itself up, and his mouth had gone dry.

Perhaps he ought to go and find Lucy. But then what would Lucy think of him, if he was too scared to open up the shower himself?

He reached out and took hold of the cubicle doorhandle. He tried to open it quietly, but it suddenly popped open with a sharp bang, and the door juddered in its frame. He took three deep breaths, and then he opened the door wide and looked inside.

A damp roll of bathroom carpet lay at the bottom of the shower-tray, covered in greyish mould.

John almost laughed in relief. But as he stepped back, he thought he glimpsed something in the mirror over the washbasin. A quick, furtive shadow – as if somebody had just been standing close behind him but had now darted out of the room.

He went back out into the corridor, and looked left and right, but there was nobody there. He called out, "Lucy? Are you OK?" but there was no reply.

He walked along to the next door and opened it. The room was gloomy, and smelled of mothballs. John was reluctant to go inside, and stayed in the corridor with his hand on the doorknob. "Hello? Mr Rogers? Is there anybody there?"

No answer. Which was hardly surprising, if he were tied up and gagged – or worse, if he were dead. John waited for a moment and then opened the door a little wider. "Hello? Mr Rogers?"

Still no answer. He cautiously stepped into the room and looked around. It was a bedroom – obviously not the master bedroom, but large enough for two single beds. The yellowish chintz curtains were drawn tight, so that the room was illuminated only by a thin, sickly light.

On one side of the room stood a huge walnut-veneered wardrobe. The veneer had been cut so that the grain formed strange wolfish faces, with knots for eyes. Even the roses on the curtains looked as if they were misshapen dwarves. Between the two beds hung a large damp-spotted etching showing a line of monks shuffling towards a ruined abbey, their faces completely concealed by their hoods.

John was about to leave the room when he saw that one of the beds had been made up completely flat, with nothing but a blanket and a single pillow on it, while the other bed was humped up, as if somebody were lying in it, sleeping.

It must be a bolster, he thought. Or maybe just a heap of bedding. But he knew that he would have to go and make sure. There was no point in looking for Mr Rogers if he didn't look everywhere.

He stood beside the bed and looked at the hump beneath the blankets. It didn't seem to be moving, so whatever it was, it wasn't asleep. He leaned closer and held his breath, in case he could hear it breathing, but there was nothing. Only the faint sound of the traffic, and Lucy, closing a bedroom door on the opposite side of the house.

He took hold of the top edge of the blanket and drew it a little way back. A bird suddenly landed on the gutter outside the bedroom window and he dropped the blanket in fright. But then he picked it up again, and slowly tugged it aside. Underneath, there was a shape swathed in linen sheets.

Please don't let it be a body, he prayed. *Whatever it is, please don't let it be a body.*

He started to unwind the sheets. Whatever was wrapped up inside them was very heavy – almost *too* heavy for a body. Yet he thought he could feel shoulders, and arms – and as he pulled back the top of the sheet he revealed something that made him feel as if cold centipedes were crawling down his back.

It was a face. An utterly white face. Its eyes were open and it was staring at him. It looked like a man in his thirties, quite handsome in a thin, unusual way, but with a sheen on his skin that wasn't at all natural, and an expression of terrible calmness that frightened John more than anything he had ever seen in his life.

He tried to say, "Lucy," but his mouth didn't seem to work.

The man continued to stare at him and said nothing. Was he alive? Was he dead? John didn't want to touch him but he didn't want to leave him, either. Supposing he jumped up from the bed and came running after him?

John leaned forward and whispered, "Are you—?" but even as he leaned forward he realized that the man was neither alive nor dead. It was a statue, an incredibly lifelike statue, with a face carved out of polished ivory.

John reached out and touched the statue's chest and under the sheets it was hard and unyielding. He knocked it and it sounded like wood. He was relieved, but all the same the statue was so realistic that he still found it unnerving.

Lucy came in. "I've looked in all of the other bedrooms," she said. "I haven't found anything except a lot of old furniture."

"Look at this," said John.

Lucy stared at the statue, startled. "He's not—?"

"No, it's made out of wood, that's all. But it scared me to death when I first took the sheet off."

"Isn't it *strange?*" said Lucy, touching its forehead with her fingertips. "I mean, who would want to make a statue like this, and then leave it lying in a bed?"

"I don't know. This whole place is strange. I keep thinking I'm seeing things."

Lucy covered up the statue's face and John replaced the blanket as he had found it. "Let's take a look at the other rooms. Then we'd better think about getting back to the office."

They went into the master bedroom, which had its own bathroom and a balcony overlooking the back garden. There were no beds in here, but only the impressions in the brown carpet where beds had once been, and a few oddly-shaped stains, like a map of Greece. The back garden was as overgrown and derelict as the front. A stone angel stood on top of a leaf-cluttered fountain, with part of her left wing missing. A half-collapsed shed was tangled with dried-up wisteria.

"It's funny, isn't it?" said Lucy. "This house is so abandoned and yet I still get the feeling that somebody lives here. I mean, I feel like I'm *trespassing.*"

They checked two smaller bedrooms, both of which were damp and sad. In one of them, the pale green paper was peeling off the wall and there was a furry grey growth up by the ceiling. In the other, a picture of Jesus hung over the bed, all the colour faded out of it by damp and sunlight.

Under the window stood a small bookcase. There were six or seven little china figurines on it, ballet dancers. Every one of them had its head broken off. On the shelf below there were several copies of the *Reader's Digest* and the carcass of a Bible with half of its pages torn out.

The bed was covered with an old pink quilt, in which John was sure that he could still see the impression of somebody's body. It was as if they might have been lying here only a few moments ago. He laid his hand on the indentation but it wasn't warm. All the same, he had the strongest feeling that they weren't alone in the house.

"Let's go," said Lucy. "There isn't anybody here. Not unless you count our wooden friend in the bedroom."

"We haven't tried the attic yet. Nor the cellar."

"I don't think I want to, either. Come on, John, or else I'm going to be late."

They walked along the upstairs corridor back towards the landing. As they did so, however, John thought that he heard a strange dragging noise coming along the corridor behind them, and he suddenly stopped and turned around.

"What's the matter?" asked Lucy.

"I don't know ... I thought I heard something."

Lucy frowned back along the corridor. "There's nobody there. It must have been your heart beating."

They continued towards the stairs, but as soon as they did so, John heard the noise again, closer this time, as if something was softly hurrying up behind them, intent on catching them before they could turn around. He stopped again, and Lucy stopped, too.

"I heard it," she said, in a voice as white as paper.

John hesitated for a moment, listening. The corridor was silent, but he had an overwhelming feeling that there were other people here, very close by, waiting for them to turn their backs.

He took hold of Lucy's hand and took a cautious step further, and then another. Then he stopped again, and listened some more.

He was sure that somebody was standing only centimetres away from him, steadily breathing, yet he couldn't see anything at all, not even a ghostly shadow.

He took another step – and, as he did so, he trod on something hard. He looked down and saw that it was a ring. He bent down and picked it up, and held it out so that Lucy could see it. A man's wedding band, made out of twin ropes of yellow and white gold.

"This is Mr Rogers' ring," John whispered.

"Are you sure about that?"

"Positive. I noticed it when I gave him the key."

"Then he must have been here, mustn't he?"

John nodded, looking around him. The atmosphere in the house, already threatening, began to tighten, as if a thunderstorm were imminent. Taking hold of Lucy's hand again, he backed slowly towards the head of the stairs, and he was conscious that they were being closely followed. He almost expected to feel breath on his cheek.

"What is it?" asked Lucy, and she was clearly terrified.

"I don't know. I don't know what it is."

"It's a *ghost*," she said. "I swear it."

"There's no such thing."

He reached behind him and felt the newel post on the top of the bannisters. "Let's make a run for it," he said. "One – two – three—"

They turned and hurtled down the stairs, taking two and three at a time. The instant they did so, they heard the someone coming after them, jumping just as fast. Lucy screamed and almost lost her balance, but she managed to grab the handrail to steady herself.

They bounded down to the hallway and ran across to the front door without looking back. John opened it up, and they rushed outside, down the steps, and out along the shingle driveway. The door slammed behind them with a deafening bang.

7

They reached Lucy's car and scrambled into it. Lucy juggled with the keys and dropped them on to the floor, but John scooped them up for her and she managed to start the engine.

"You're right!" John panted. "It *is* haunted! I don't believe in ghosts but there's a ghost in there!"

"Let's just go," said Lucy. She swerved out into the road, nearly knocking an old man off his bicycle. "Oi!" he shouted after them.

They sped through the mid-morning traffic back to Streatham High Road. "We'll have to take this ring to the police," said John.

"Oh, yes. And where are you going to say that you found it?"

"What are you talking about? I'm going to tell them the truth, that's all."

"And what do you think Mr Vane's going to do when he finds out that we've borrowed his key and gone snooping around one of his precious houses? He's going to sack us, that's what. And I don't know about you, but I need this job."

"So what else can we do? Mr Rogers could still be in the house somewhere, couldn't he? He could still be alive. What if he starves to death, because we were too scared to tell the police?"

"We could give them an anonymous tip-off," Lucy suggested. "You know, like they do on *Crimewatch*."

John held up Mr Rogers' ring and inspected it from all angles. "I suppose we could. And we could find out more about 66 Mountjoy Avenue, too. Mr Vane must have some kind of file on it."

"You're not going to start *rifling* again, are you? You're going to get yourself in terrible trouble."

John didn't say anything. He was thinking about the thing that had followed them down the empty corridor, and the statue lying on the bed. He couldn't get the statue's pale ivory face out of his mind – its unblinking stare; its eerie, terrifying calm. He wondered if it were the statue of a real man, or if the sculptor simply created the most frightening face he could think of.

During his lunchbreak, he went out to a callbox on the corner of Fernwood Avenue and dialled 999. An old woman in a flowery dress arrived outside just as his call was being answered, and she continued to glare at him all the way through his conversation.

"Emergency. Which service, please?"

"I want to talk to somebody about Mr Rogers who's gone missing in Streatham."

There was a pause. The old woman glared at him so he turned his back on her.

"Streatham CID, Detective Sergeant Bynoe speaking."

"Oh, yes. It's that missing man who was on the telly last night. Mr Rogers. I saw him going into 66 Mountjoy Avenue yesterday dinnertime and I didn't see him come out again."

"Who are you?"

"An anonymous caller."

"Well, why don't you stop being anonymous and tell me who you are? There could be a reward in this."

"No, that's all right. I'm just giving you a tip-off, that's all."

"Was Mr Rogers alone when you saw him?"

"I don't know."

"What do you mean, you don't know? Either he was or he wasn't."

"Well, I didn't exactly see him go into the house with my actual eyes."

"Then how do you know he went into the house?"

"I just do, that's all."

"I'd like to know how."

"He dropped his wedding ring. Either that, or somebody pulled it off."

"Where did he drop it?"

"In the house, of course. That's how I know that he was definitely there."

"So you've been in the house subsequent to Mr Rogers going there?"

"I can't tell you."

"Listen, Mr Anonymous Caller, I think that you and I need to have a little chat, don't you? Why don't you stay where you are and I'll send a car round to collect you."

"You don't know where I am."

"Of course I do. You're in the callbox on the corner of Fernwood Avenue. I've got an officer on his way to see you already."

John dropped the phone as if it had suddenly burst into flame. He pushed his way out of the callbox and ran across the road. The old woman called out, "Kids of today! 'Ooligans, that's what! 'Ooligans, the 'ole lot of them!"

John was out of breath by the time he got back to the office. Courtney was waiting for him impatiently. "Where have you been? I have to meet a client in five minutes."

"Sorry."

"You will be, if I lose this sale. Make some copies

of these floor-plans for me, would you, while I'm gone."

John was left in the office on his own. He copied Courtney's documents and then he made himself a cup of coffee and walked back to his desk with four chocolate biscuits in his mouth at once. He started to drink his coffee with a loud slurping noise (it was hot, and anyway there was nobody else to hear him) but he couldn't keep his eyes off the door to Mr Vane's room. Mr Vane must have a file on 66 Mountjoy Avenue – and he must know all about the statue, too. Perhaps he was aware that the house was haunted, and that was why he never let anybody handle it except him. Perhaps *all* the houses on his special list were haunted.

He went across to Mr Vane's door and put his hand on the doorknob. No, better not. He might get caught, and Mr Vane wouldn't be so forgiving a second time. It had been risky enough this morning. If Mr Cleat had emerged from the toilet just two seconds earlier, he would have bumped into Lucy sneaking out of Mr Vane's room after putting the key back.

He sat down and finished his coffee. He brushed crumbs from his desk. He looked across at Mr Vane's door. He doodled a cartoon of Mr Cleat with an enormous nose. He looked back at Mr Vane's door.

The next thing he knew, he was sliding open one of Mr Vane's filing cabinets, and rifling through the sour-smelling old documents inside it.

He couldn't find anything in the top drawer, just a lot of old brochures dating back to the 1920s. There was a brand new house for sale in Tooting for £236, but that was in 1924. He tried the second drawer, and that was filled with newspapers, some of them so old that they were dark brown.

In the bottom drawer, however, together with a half-bottle of gin and a pot of glue, he found a large black folder. He lifted out the folder, laid it on one of the few clear spaces on Mr Vane's desk, and opened it. Inside, there were particulars for over a dozen houses. Some of them were obviously years old, but two or three of them were brand new, with glossy photographs stuck to them.

Here it was – 66 Mountjoy Avenue. *A spacious character residence ideal for the larger family. Price on application.* No mention of ivory-faced statues, however, or invisible presences that breathed over your face and chased you down the stairs. But there was a handwritten list of previous owners, and the dates they had lived there. The last time the house had been occupied was four months ago, by Mr and Mrs W. Bennett. Before them it was Mr and Mrs K. Dadarchanji; and before them, Mr and Mrs G.L. Geoffreys.

What struck John was that none of the previous owners had lived in the house for longer than a year, and some of them had moved out within two or three months of moving in. Hardly surprising, he thought, if the owners had experienced the same kind of spooky manifestations as he and Lucy had.

He made a note of all of the addresses in the folder. There was a scattering of local addresses – 113 Greyhound Road; 7 Laverdale Square; 14 Ullswater Road; The Larches, Blackwood Avenue. But surprisingly, most of the properties were located miles away. 93 Madeira Terrace, Brighton. Carstairs House, Pennine Road, Preston. There were even houses in Wales and Scotland.

He heard a noise in the office outside. Quickly, he shuffled the particulars back into the folder and returned it to its drawer. He was darting towards the door when it suddenly opened. He managed to dodge behind it and press himself against the panelling. Mr Cleat came in, dropped a file on Mr Vane's desk, and went out again. John waited until he heard Mr Cleat go into the kitchen before he crept out and closed Mr Vane's door behind him.

Mr Cleat reappeared. "Where have you been? I thought I told you never to leave the office unattended."

"I've been here all the time."

"You've been *where* all the time?"

"Here."

Mr Cleat gave an irritable tut. "I want you to run an errand for me. I want you to take these papers along to Hawthorn & Black, the solicitors. They're in Norbury, so you'll have to take the bus."

John was quite glad to get out of the office. It was a warm, windy afternoon and the skies above the suburbs were filled with the sort of clouds that looked like dogs, or castles, or fat recumbent giants. Before he caught the bus he bought a chocolate Cornetto and took it on to the top deck, right at the front.

It didn't take him long to deliver Mr Cleat's package. He walked back along the main road, looking in all of the shop windows. He stopped for a while to watch the tropical fish in Norbury Aquatics.

As he was crossing a side turning, however, his attention was caught by a small crowd of people outside a demolition site. There were three police vans there, too, along with two lorries and a clutter of other cars, and a long white Metropolitan Police caravan marked *Incident Unit*.

John looked at his watch. He had plenty of time. He walked into the square and joined the crowd, although he couldn't see anything much. He asked one man what was going on but the man simply shrugged and said, "I dunno."

John walked up to the police tape and tried to peer over the plywood hoardings, but they were too high. He climbed on to the low brick wall in front of the house next door and then he could see the remains of the half-demolished house and over a dozen police officers in shirtsleeves milling around in front of it.

"Hoi, what are you up to?" shouted one of them, walking towards him.

"Nothing. Just taking a look."

"Well, there's nothing to see, so 'op it."

"What's happened?" he asked.

"Don't you watch the news?"

"Sometimes. What's happened?"

"They were knocking this house down and they found some skeletons in it. More than fifty, that's how many they've brought out so far."

John stayed and watched for a little longer, in case they brought another skeleton out, but after a while he got bored. He bought an *Evening Standard* and took the bus back to the office.

The Norbury "house of bones" story was on page five. He vaguely remembered hearing something about it on the radio but he hadn't really paid any attention. But when he read the second paragraph of the story he felt a prickling sensation all the way up his neck.

"The skeletons of more than fifty people have now been recovered from the house in Norbury, south London, where demolition workers broke into a bricked-up room on Monday and discovered heaps of human bones.

"Number 7 Laverdale Square had been the subject of a compulsory purchase order to make way for a new road-widening scheme. The last owners, Dr and Mrs Philip Lister, vacated the property over six months ago without leaving a forwarding address, and police are anxious to talk to them.

"A next-door neighbour, Mrs Anne Finch, said that she and other residents of Laverdale Square believed the house had 'a bad atmosphere' and that sometimes she had heard 'wailing and shouting' coming from the house during the night – 'terrible great shouts, like a man roaring through a megaphone'.

"She had also heard thunderous footsteps, as if people were running up and down uncarpeted stairs.

" 'I was glad when I heard the place was going to be knocked down,' she said. 'Now they've discovered all these skeletons. It's horrible.' "

John lowered the paper, feeling breathless. *Number 7, Laverdale Square.* That was one of the houses on Mr Vane's list! And it had "*a bad atmosphere,*" just like 66 Mountjoy Avenue. He had felt it for himself. And he had heard strange noises, too. How much of a coincidence could it be that *two* of Mr Vane's special properties had such a threatening feeling about them?

There was no question about it. He should go and look at some more houses on the special list, and see if they were just as threatening.

8

As he was about to step off the bus, he saw two police cars parked right outside Blight, Simpson & Vane. Immediately he thought, *Oh, no! They've found out that I made that anonymous phone call.* He didn't know whether to go back into the office and brazen it out, or stay on the bus and go home.

"Make your mind up," said the bus conductor. "We're supposed to be back at the depot by the end of August."

He took a deep breath, jumped off the bus, and went into the office. Inside, he found two plainclothes detectives talking to Mr Vane and Mr Cleat. Mr Cleat gave him a sharp *where-have-you-been?* look, but didn't say anything. Mr Vane was saying, "We have the property on our books, yes, but the owners are no longer with us."

"Dead?" asked Inspector Carter.

"Oh, good Lord, no. Torremolinos. Mr Anderson's arthritis, don't you know. He needed the sun."

"Can you think of any reason why anybody should have suggested that Mr Rogers was still there?"

"Not at all. I suppose it may have been a practical joke."

"If it was, I don't think it's particularly funny, do you?"

"No, I don't. Unless it was a competitor, trying to stir up trouble for me."

"Oh, yes? And why should they want to do that?"

Mr Vane gave one of his yellow grins. "Estate agency isn't as dull as it appears, Inspector. There's plenty of cut and thrust. Agencies stealing each other's clients from under their noses – agencies undercutting each other's percentages."

"Sounds like pretty hair-raising stuff," said Carter.

"Oh, it can be, it can be. And people do bear grudges."

Carter flipped open his notebook. "So Mr Rogers came in here, borrowed the key to 66 Mountjoy Avenue, and went off to look at it? But when you came back to the office, Mr Cleat, and discovered what had happened, you went after him, to stop him?"

"That's right. 66 Mountjoy Avenue isn't yet fit for inspection. I would have been doing the owners a disservice if I had let Mr Rogers see it in that condition."

"So he didn't actually enter the property?"

"Absolutely not, no."

John could feel Mr Rogers' ring in his pocket, and he was tempted to bring it out and show that Mr Cleat was telling a lie, but Lucy must have read his mind. She gave him a quick shake of her head and mouthed the word "no".

Inspector Carter said, "Who dealt with Mr Rogers when he came to pick up the key?"

"Young John here. It was his first day. He shouldn't really have given him the key – but Mr Rogers was very insistent."

"Get into trouble, did you, John?" asked Carter.

"Mr Vane was very understanding," put in Mr Cleat, before John could answer.

Carter said, "What sort of a state was he in, Mr Rogers? Was he agitated, at all? Or anxious?"

"He was normal, that's all," John told him. "He was in a hurry, you know. But he didn't look worried or anything."

"So he didn't look as if he was going to top himself? Drown himself, or throw himself in front of a train?"

John shook his head.

"All right, then," said Carter, putting his notebook back in his pocket. "Thanks for your co-operation, Mr Vane. I think you're probably right. Whoever made that phone call was just trying to stir up a bit of trouble for you."

Mr Vane gave him another grin. "Believe me, Inspector, if I ever find out who it was, I'll wring his neck for him."

At four o'clock, Mr Vane and Mr Cleat left the office together. As soon as they had gone, John took out the ring.

"What's that?" asked Liam. "You're not going to propose to me, are you?"

"It's Mr Rogers' wedding ring. We found it at 66 Mountjoy Avenue. So Mr Cleat was telling a lie."

Liam came over and examined the ring closely. "Are you sure that's his? Why didn't you tell the police about it?"

"What, and get the sack?" said Lucy.

"Lucy's right," said Courtney. "And apart from that, Cleaty and the police are like *this*—" he crossed his fingers. "He's a mason and a Rotarian and member of the Neighbourhood Watch committee. If he says that Mr Rogers didn't go into the house, and you say he did, who do you think the police are going to believe?"

"You need more evidence," said Liam.

"Well, I think there's something really weird going on with Mr Vane's special list," said John. "You know that house where they've found all those skeletons? That was one of Mr Vane's houses, too."

"That house in Norbury? I hadn't realized that."

"Number 7, Laverdale Square," said Courtney. "The council bought it because they wanted to widen the road. Don't you remember? Mr Vane was in a terrible temper about it for weeks."

"You're not trying to say that *he* killed all of those people?" said Lucy. "I know he's a bit scary, but he doesn't look like a mass murderer."

"I think he looks *exactly* like a mass murderer," said Liam.

John said, "I went into his office and I copied out the whole of the special list. I think we ought to go and look at some of the other houses."

"Oh, come on," said Courtney. "If Mr Vane had anything to hide, he would have kept the list and the keys locked up in the safe."

"Perhaps he didn't think that anybody would ever suspect him," said Lucy. "I mean, those skeletons were all hidden in the walls, weren't they? If the council hadn't knocked the house down, who would have ever found out?"

"It's much more likely he didn't know anything about it," Courtney replied. "And it's much more likely that Mr Rogers went into the house, dropped his ring, and then disappeared somewhere else."

"If he did that, why did Cleaty lie to the police?"

"I don't know," said Courtney, "and I can't say that I particularly care. This is all a lot of wild speculation, that's all."

"I'm still going to go and look at Mr Vane's other houses," John declared. "There's one in Brighton – 93 Madeira Terrace. I'll go down on Saturday."

"Well, there's a coincidence," said Liam. "I'm going to Brighton for the racing on Saturday afternoon. We could go down together."

"That would be *great*," said John.

"Don't let Liam persuade you to put any money on the horses," Courtney warned him. "You'll end up bankrupt before you've even earned anything."

They sped down to Brighton early on Saturday morning in Liam's Golf GTi. The sun was shining and it was warm enough to drive with the roof down. John had borrowed a pair of sunglasses from his sister Ruth which pinched his nose. He felt scruffy. He wished he had a black polo shirt and a pair of chinos like Liam, instead of his grey, washed-out jeans and his saggy maroon top. But his spirits lifted as they drove up over the South Downs, through Devil's Dyke, and he could see the farms and fields of mid-Sussex spread out behind him, and the English Channel glittering in front.

They drove along the seafront, past the Palace Pier, and along Marine Parade. John felt almost as if he were on holiday. "Should have brought our buckets and spades," said Liam, cheerfully.

Madeira Terrace was a dark, steep street on the borders of Hove, and out of sight of the sea. It was lined on both sides with narrow, four-storey terraced houses, built of hard red brick. Each house had a small walled garden in front, but very few of them were well tended. Most of them were cluttered with broken bicycles and bent dustbins and crumpled newspapers. Liam parked in front of a Dormobile with flat tyres and tugged on the handbrake hard. "This is it. Number 93. Looks as if it's empty."

The windows were dark and filmed over with dust. The blue paint on the front door was peeling. There was a small crowd of empty milk bottles on the step, and the letterbox was crammed with circulars.

John and Liam climbed out of the car and went up to the front door. John pressed the doorbell and heard it buzz faintly like a bluebottle in a jar. They waited, and tried the bell again, but nobody answered.

"Right," said Liam. "It looks as if we'll have to try a different approach."

"What do you mean? We can't break in."

"Of course we can break in. The property's empty and we're the sole agents. There's nothing illegal in making an inspection."

"Well, all right," said John, uncertainly, looking up and down the street. There was nobody in sight except for an old woman toiling up the incline with a tartan shopping trolley.

Liam went back to the car and returned with a black leather case. "Lock-picks," he explained. "I took a locksmith's course, once upon a time. I was going to follow my dad into the hardware business. I did some work for a couple of estate agents and then I realized that they were making ten times more money than I was."

He fiddled around with the door for a while, and then abruptly opened it. He pushed back all the papers and letters that were stacked up behind it and stepped inside. "Smells damp. It could do with an airing."

John waited on the doorstep. He didn't like the house at all. It smelled not only of damp, but of decay: of dry rot and dust and something else, too – something deeply unpleasant, like blocked drains, or rotting seaweed, all tangled up with dead dogfish.

"I don't know, Liam," he said, cautiously.

"Come on, will you?" Liam encouraged him. "It was your idea, after all. And I agree with you. Ever since I first worked for Mr Vane I thought that he was up to something queer. Now we can find out what it is."

John hesitated a moment longer, and then he

stepped inside. The house was in a desperate state of repair. The wallpaper was peeling off the walls like dead skin, and there were spots and smudges of mould on the ceiling. The house was unfurnished and uncarpeted, and as they walked along the narrow corridor to the kitchen at the back, their footsteps echoed flatly in every room.

The kitchen overlooked a small, dark yard, overgrown with weeds. Liam opened the larder but there was nothing in it except an ancient packet of Scott's Porridge Oats and a spattering of rat droppings. John turned the tap over the stainless steel sink but there was no water.

"So what are we looking for?" said Liam, as they went back through to the sitting-room. There were dusty rectangular marks on the walls where pictures had once hung. "Mr Vane is up to something or other with all of these properties, but what?"

"I don't know," said John. "But 66 Mountjoy Avenue felt like this, too. You know – it had the same kind of horrible atmosphere."

"Most empty houses have a horrible atmosphere," Liam told him. "It isn't houses that make homes, it's the people who live in them. Houses, on their own, are nothing at all. They're dead."

They looked around the tiny dining-room. A single fork lay on the floor, as if somebody had dropped it years and years ago and never bothered to pick it up.

They climbed the steep, uncarpeted stairs. "You'd never guess it, but this is a good sound property," said Liam. "Some attention to the roof, and a lick of paint, and you could get a good price for this."

"I wouldn't buy it if you paid me," said John. He was beginning to wish that he had never come.

They looked into the bathroom and all the bedrooms. Empty, their bare walls patterned with fingerprints and screw-holes and Sellotape marks. In one of the smallest rooms, a cut-out picture of a teddy bear still remained, stuck to the side of the fireplace.

"Well," said Liam. "That's it. Nothing here at all, as far as I can see."

They were about to go back downstairs when John thought he heard a footstep in one of the bedrooms.

"Stop," he said. "Did you hear that?"

"Did I hear what?" asked Liam.

They waited and listened, and then they heard another footstep, and another. There was no doubt about it. Somebody was walking across the bare boarded floor.

"John, you wait here," Liam cautioned him. He tiptoed across the landing and gently nudged open the bedroom door. From where he was standing, John couldn't see anything, only the bedroom window, and a dark horse-chestnut tree outside.

Liam went into the room and the door swung back.

John waited for almost a minute. Then he called, "Liam? What's going on?"

There was no answer. "Liam?" John repeated. "Come on, Liam, stop messing about. Let's go."

Still no answer. John went over to the bedroom door and opened it a little way. "Liam?"

He looked around the door and what he saw he couldn't immediately understand. He felt as if his entire skin surface was prickling and his stomach was tightening up into a tennis ball.

"*Liam?*"

Liam was kneeling on the other side of the room. Except that it wasn't all of Liam. Half of his head had disappeared into the wall, so that all John could see of it was his right eye and his right nostril and the right side of his mouth, dragged wide open in agony. His left arm had disappeared and most of his chest, too. His left knee had gone, but his left foot was still free, even though it was trembling uncontrollably, like the hoof of a recently-shot stag.

John stood and stared at him in horror. Then he hurried over and crouched down beside him and shouted, "Liam! What's happening to you? What can I do?"

Liam grasped frantically for John's hand. He was tense, tight, shivering. "Help me," he croaked. "Help me, John, for the love of God. It's pulling me in." John grabbed hold of his arm, but Liam was being sucked into the flowery-patterned wallpaper as smoothly and steadily as if he were being sucked into quicksand. John pulled at him, lodging his feet against the skirting board to give himself as much leverage as he could, and for a moment he thought that he had managed to stop Liam from going into the wallpaper any further.

"Get me out, John," Liam begged him. "You have to get me out of here."

But then his head was pulled even deeper into the wall, and his mouth disappeared with a last choking cough. The last that John saw of his face was his single right eye, as green as glass, staring at him in absolute terror. Then that too was gone.

"*Liam!*" he screamed at him. "*Liam!*"

He wrenched at Liam's polo shirt, but all he succeeded in doing was tearing the collar. He wrenched again and again, but Liam's chest disappeared, and then his shoulder, and then his legs. At the very last, John was pulling at nothing but his arm, but that was sucked in, too, right up to the wrist. For a few seconds his hand reached out of the wall, his fingers splayed wide as if he were still pleading to be rescued. Then even that was gone, and the wall was bare.

John stood up, so shocked and shaky that he had to lean against the wall to regain his balance. But he felt something stir beneath his hand — something that seemed to *crawl* right underneath the wallpaper.

He rushed down the stairs so quickly that he lost his footing and had to snatch at the handrail to stop himself from falling. He ran into the street and stopped, circling wildly around and around, panting in terror. *What was he going to do? What was he going to do?* There was nobody in sight, as if all the residents of Madeira Terrace knew what was happening, and stayed well away.

He ran a little way up the hill but then he stopped and went down again. He stood by the gate but he was too frightened to go back into the house. What was he going to do? Call the police? But who was going to believe that Liam had vanished into the wall? The police would probably think that *he* had murdered Liam and buried his body somewhere.

He couldn't think of anybody else he could call. They shouldn't have been trespassing in the house in the first place, so he couldn't expect any help from Mr Cleat. The only thing he could do was get away from Brighton as quickly as possible and go back home.

He could have driven Liam's car, but Liam had the keys, wherever he was, and John didn't know how to hot-wire it. He kept pacing up and down outside the house, fretful and undecided. There was one thing he knew: he didn't want to go back in. Whatever had taken Liam could just as easily take him too.

John began to walk uphill, in the direction of Brighton station. When he reached the top of Madeira Terrace, he began to run, and he didn't stop running until the station concourse came into sight.

9

He called Lucy and said, "Liam's gone."

"What do you mean, 'Liam's gone'?"

"Something terrible's happened. I have to see you right away."

"I can't. I'm supposed to be going out with my boyfriend at eight."

"Lucy, I have to see you! I just have to see you!"

"Come on, John. This isn't a weekday at work, when I've got nothing better to do. This is Saturday night."

"Lucy, don't you understand me? Liam's *dead*. At least I *think* he's dead."

"What? What do you mean, dead? You're joking."

"We went into the house in Brighton and he was sucked right into the wall."

"Oh, for goodness' sake, John. You had me worried there for a moment. Now listen, I'm in a hurry. Paul's coming round in a minute and we're going to Volts."

"Lucy, listen. It's the truth. Liam was sucked right into the wall and now he's dead."

There was a very long silence. In the background, John could hear pop music playing. Eventually Lucy said, "This isn't a wind-up, is it? I know what Liam's like."

"It's true," he told her. There were tears in his eyes and he could barely speak. "I don't know how it happened but it's true."

"You'd better come round then, as quick as you can. Where are you?"

"Streatham Common station."

"In that case, I'll come and get you."

When Lucy arrived outside the station she was all dressed up in a short purple dress and dangly hoop earrings. She smelled strongly of some musky perfume. "I'm sorry," said John, as he climbed into the car. "I couldn't think of anybody else to call."

She looked at him seriously. He was very pale and puffy-eyed. "You're sure Liam's dead?"

"He must be. It happened right in front of my eyes. The same thing must have happened to Mr Rogers. The same thing must have happened to all of those people at Laverdale Square. Mr Vane's houses can suck people in."

They had stopped at the top of Greyhound Lane. Lucy turned to John and her face was bathed in red light from the stop signal. "This isn't a joke, is it?" she asked him. "This isn't you and Liam pulling my leg? Because if it is, I'll never forgive you."

John started to cry. He was desperately embarrassed but the shock of what had happened to Liam was too much for him. Tears dripped down his cheeks and his throat was so choked up that he could hardly breathe. Lucy reached over and squeezed his hand and said, "I believe you. Don't worry. I believe you."

She drove him home. His mother was sitting in the living-room in her dressing-gown, and his father was feeding her with Horlicks. Bruce Willis was flickering across the television screen but they weren't really watching.

"Dad – Mum – this is Lucy, from work."

"How do you do, Lucy," said his father. "There's some Horlicks to spare, if you'd like some."

"Um, no thanks," said Lucy.

"John, you're looking a bit peaky," said his mother, out of the side of her mouth. "What about something to eat?"

"No thanks, Mum, honestly."

John took Lucy to his bedroom. As they went upstairs, he heard his father saying, "Nice to see

John bringing a girl home." John thought, *if only you knew why*.

John sat down on the bed. "What's the matter with your mum?" Lucy asked him, looking at all his football posters.

"Oh. She had a stroke. Dad has to do everything now. Well, Dad and me. My sister's always out."

"Sounds tough," Lucy said, sympathetically. John shrugged. "So what are we going to do about Liam, then?" she continued.

"I don't know. I thought about calling the police but suppose they don't believe me? I mean, suppose they think *I* did it?"

"Why should they think that?"

"Because I was the last person to see him alive, wasn't I? He's gone missing but they won't be able to find his body and they're bound to think it was me."

"All right, all right, calm down," said Lucy. "Just tell me again how it happened."

John pressed his hand flat against his bedroom wall. "He was just sucked in. I couldn't believe it. I still can't believe it now."

Lucy thought for a moment, and then she said, "If you're really worried that the police are going to think it was you, you're going to need some evidence, aren't you, to prove that it wasn't? I think we ought to go down there. Down to Brighton, I mean. I think we ought to knock down the wall and see if we can find Liam's bones."

"Liam's *bones*?"

"Listen, John, if the house in Brighton is the same as the house in Norbury, then that's the explanation for all of those skeletons, isn't it?"

"I don't get what you mean."

"They said on the news that the skeletons were all bricked up, didn't they? But the bricks were really old and some of the skeletons were new."

"So perhaps they weren't bricked up at all," said John. "They were sucked through the wall, the same as Liam."

"Exactly. So why don't we go down there tomorrow and take a look?"

John shook his head. "I don't want to go back there, Lucy. I really don't."

"I don't blame you. But I don't see what choice we've got."

"You should have seen Liam's face. It was horrible."

Lucy sat down beside him and took hold of his hand. "If we don't do it, then the chances are that Mr Vane will get away with it. All he has to do is say that he didn't know anything about it, and what can they charge him with then? But if we can prove that *all* of his houses are the same, and that he *knew*..."

Finally, John nodded. Lucy had managed to calm him down a little. All the same, he couldn't stop himself from picturing Liam's one green eye, staring at him in utter desperation before it was dragged right into the wall. He knew that he would remember that eye for the rest of his life.

They caught the train to Brighton because Lucy didn't fancy driving all that way. It started to rain when they reached Haywards Heath and by the time they came out of Brighton station it was pouring. They took a taxi to Madeira Terrace and told the driver to stop by Liam's car.

"What a dump," said Lucy, looking up at the house. "Let's go inside before we get soaked."

They stood in the porch and John tried the door. "Locked," he said. "Liam opened it with a lock-pick." He had brought his father's hammer with him in a Sainsbury's bag but he didn't want to break a window.

"Try the old credit-card trick."

"I haven't got a credit card."

Lucy took out her Barclaycard and tried to slide it down the gap in the front door to release the latch, but she couldn't force it in far enough. John stepped out into the rain and peered into the sitting-room windows. He tried rattling them, and one of them seemed loose. "Look, the catch isn't fastened. If I can find a lever or something..."

There was a rusty gate hinge lying in the front garden. He picked it up and wedged it into the bottom of the window frame. The window was jammed with years of paint, but at last he managed to lift it a centimetre clear of the sill. Another pull, and it was open.

"Anybody around?" he asked Lucy.

Lucy shook her head. "You should have been a burglar, instead of an estate agent."

John didn't say anything. He was so frightened about going back inside the house that his mouth was all dry. He hesitated for a moment, and then he climbed through the window into the musty-smelling sitting-room. Then he went around to the front door to let Lucy in. She sniffed and said, "I'm not surprised you didn't want to come back here. It's horrible."

"Just be careful of the walls," John warned her.

He led her up the stairs to the landing. Outside they could see the rain sweeping in from the sea, and the grey clouds rushing over the Brighton rooftops like a pack of mad dogs.

"This is the room," said John, and he was actually shaking.

"Did Liam say anything before he was sucked into the wall?"

"Nothing. Nothing at all."

Lucy eased the door open and looked inside. It was very gloomy in there, and the rain dribbling down the windows made it seem even more depressing and threatening.

"It was over there," said John, pointing to the place in the wall where Liam had disappeared.

Lucy approached it and stared at it closely. "You can't *see* anything, can you?" She reached out to touch it but John said, *"Don't!"*

"All right, then. Try knocking off some of the plaster."

John took the hammer out of the bag and went up to the wall. The plaster was dead, and his first blow made a deep circular dent. He hit the wall again, and then again, and a large lump of plaster dropped off and scattered across the floorboards.

He swung at the wall for over five minutes, until he had exposed the plaster right the way down to the brick. His hammering made so much noise that every now and then he stopped to listen, in case he had disturbed the neighbours next door. But Madeira Terrace was as wet and silent as a neglected graveyard, and if anybody had heard him, they obviously didn't care.

"Nothing," he said. "I'm beginning to feel like I imagined it."

"Liam's car is still outside, and Liam's car is his pride and joy. That's how I know you didn't imagine it."

John said, "Maybe the wall sucked him in completely. Maybe there's nothing left."

"The skeletons they found in the Norbury house were hidden behind the bricks. Why don't you try pulling a few out?"

John banged away at the bricks for a few minutes

more, and at last he succeeded in dislodging one of them. After that it was easy to pull out another four or five. He peered inside the cavity. It was completely black, and there was a faint draught blowing up it.

"See anything?" asked Lucy.

John shook his head.

"Let me put my hand in and feel."

"You can't! Supposing it starts to suck you in, too?"

"Then you can pull me back out again."

"I couldn't pull Liam back out. The wall was much too strong."

Lucy knelt down beside him and looked into the cavity, too. "Too dark. We should have brought a torch. Here – give me that hammer for a moment."

She cautiously poked the hammer into the cavity and moved it from side to side. Almost immediately, John heard a *clokkk!* noise and Lucy said, "I've hit something – there's something here!"

"Be careful," John cautioned her. "Don't put your hand in, whatever you do."

"It's all right, I can catch it with the hammer."

With great care, Lucy manoeuvred the hammer around until she had hooked whatever it was that she had found. Slowly, she lifted it upward, until they could see what it was.

"Oh, no," John whispered.

Suspended on the end of the hammer, with the

claw through its eye-socket, was a human skull. It had no flesh or hair on it at all, and it shone white as if it had been polished.

Lucy brought it out of the wall. Her hands were shaking so much that she dropped it on the floor, and it rolled a little way across the floorboards. It rocked noisily backwards and forwards and then it lay still.

They both stepped away from it. It looked as if it were grinning at a private joke. Lucy clasped her hand over her mouth, her eyes wide with shock.

"It's Liam," said John. "It's Liam – it must be Liam."

"Oh God, it's horrible," said Lucy. "It's horrible, I can't believe it!"

John said, "Let's go – come on, let's go." He had seen plenty of skulls before – in museums, in the biology lab at school – but not the skull of somebody he knew. "Come on, we don't need any more evidence, let's go."

But Lucy went back to the cavity and peered inside. "There are more bones in there. Lots of them. I can see them now."

"It doesn't matter," said John, without taking his eyes off the skull. "Let's just leave everything like it is and call the police."

"All right," Lucy agreed, without any hesitation. She stood up and looked around her. "Just imagine. If this is the same as the Norbury house there could be dozens of skeletons in every wall. The whole house could be *crammed* with them."

John ushered her out of the room and hurriedly down the stairs. He couldn't get out of the house fast enough. Before he slammed the front door shut he gave one quick glance over his shoulder. He had a hideous feeling that Liam's skull would be at the top of the stairs, following them, but of course it wasn't.

They had just reached the front gate when an elderly man in a flat cap came out of the house next door.

"You're not thinking of buying the place, are you?" he asked, a roll-up cigarette waggling on his lower lip.

"Oh, no. We were just looking."

"Well, let me give you a word of advice. That place is better off empty."

"Oh, yes?" asked Lucy. "Why's that?"

"It's an unhappy house, that's why. I've seen seven or eight families come and go from that house, and it's always the same. They arrive cheerful and then before you know it they're screaming blue murder at each other. Running up and down stairs and shouting like mad people. Then they pack up and that's it."

"Well, we'll take your advice," said Lucy.

"You do that. You don't want to end up like them, all that roaring and running up and down stairs. You'd think there was fifty of them sometimes, instead of five."

"It's so scary," said Lucy as they hurried up the street. "You know I didn't really believe you at first."

John stopped. The rain had eased off now, and the ghost of a sun had appeared behind the clouds. "I think we should call the police now. The sooner the better."

"You look awful," said Lucy.

"I feel awful. I mean, this is not just some kind of trick, is it? It really happened. He really got dragged into the wall."

"Let's find a café. We can have a cup of tea or something and you can call the police from there."

"I should have saved Liam. I tried my best, but I couldn't."

"Stop blaming yourself," said Lucy, taking hold of his arm. Together they walked down to Queen's Road as stiffly and as mechanically as if they had just walked away from a plane crash.

They found a little café just opposite the station. Its windows were all steamed up and it was crowded with bus drivers and cabbies. John went up to the counter to order two cups of tea while Lucy sat down at a table close to the telephone.

"Eighty pence, love," said the red-faced woman behind the counter. John reached into his jeans pocket for his wallet. It wasn't there. He tried his jacket pockets and it wasn't there either. He turned to Lucy in desperation.

"My wallet – I must have dropped it in the house. It's got everything in it. All my money, everything."

"Do you want this tea or not?" the red-faced woman demanded.

Lucy came up to the counter and paid for it. "We'll just have to go back," she said, unhappily.

It took them ten minutes to walk back to Madeira Terrace and they walked in silence. When they reached the house, they looked at each other and they still couldn't put the dread that they were feeling into words. John opened the gate and went into the front garden. "I'll try to be as quick as I can. But if anything goes wrong – you know – I'll shout out."

"Just stay away from the walls," said Lucy.

John eased up the sitting-room window and climbed awkwardly back into the house. There was the same musty smell, and he had the same awful sense that something was waiting for him. He glanced back at Lucy and gave her a hesitant wave. Then, with his heart drumming, he stepped into the hallway.

The first thing he did was look up the stairs, to see if the skull really *had* tried to follow him, but of course the landing was empty. He quickly searched the hallway itself but his wallet wasn't there. He must have dropped it up in the bedroom when he was knocking that hole in the wall.

He climbed the stairs as quietly as he could. The fifth stair let out a low groan, almost as if it were human, and he stopped and listened for nearly ten seconds, holding his breath. He heard nothing more, except the seagulls crying in the wind outside, and so he carefully continued until he reached the landing.

He entered the bedroom – and there, to his relief, he saw his wallet lying on the floor, close to the skirting board. But with a tingle of fear and bewilderment, he saw that the skull had disappeared.

Not only that, the hole in the wall was patched up. Not so much patched up as *healed*, so that even the faded wallpaper had closed over itself, like skin.

He heard a creak in the attic above his head. He scooped up his wallet and this time he was out of the house so fast that he bruised his shoulder against the front doorframe. He didn't even stop to open the garden gate, but jumped straight over the wall.

"Come on!" he panted, snatching at Lucy's sleeve. He began to run up the road and she came running after him.

"John, stop! What's the matter? John, I can't keep this up!"

John slowed down to a hurried walking pace.

"It's gone! I went up into the bedroom and it's gone!"

"What's gone? What are you talking about?"

"The skull, that's what's gone. Liam's skull. And the wall – it looks like we never knocked a hole in it at all."

She had to skip once or twice to keep up with him. "The skull can't be gone – not unless somebody's taken it, and who would want to do a thing like that?"

"I don't know. But I don't like this at all."

"Well, let's go back to the café and call the police."

"And say what? We haven't got any evidence now, have we? And we'll sound like we're mad. Well, perhaps we *are* mad. Perhaps we're having hallucinations."

"John, you know very well that we *did* go into the house and we *did* knock a hole in the wall and we *did* find Liam's skull."

"I don't know. I don't know. I've got to think about this."

"All right, then. Let's go back home and think about it. But we can't just forget about it, can we? We can't just pretend it never happened."

They had nearly reached the station when John had the oddest feeling that somebody was following them. He stopped, and turned around, but there were so many people walking up and down Queen's

Road, some of them still carrying umbrellas, that he couldn't be sure. Yet he thought he glimpsed a man in a dark coat step quickly into a shop doorway, as if to avoid being seen.

"What's wrong?" asked Lucy.

"I don't know. Nothing."

They carried on walking, but then John turned around again, and this time, for a split-second, he saw the man in the dark coat for a second time. Almost immediately, though, the man vanished behind an umbrella and when John searched for his face again, he had gone.

But even in a split-second, there was no mistaking that face. It was pale as ivory and utterly calm. *It was the face of the sculpture that John had found on the bed at 66 Mountjoy Avenue.*

10

"It *can't* have been," said Lucy, as the train sped through the Surrey countryside and back to the suburbs. "You've just got the ab–dabs, that's all."

"It was. It was the same face. I swear it."

Lucy shook her head and turned to look out of the window. They were both tired now and feeling fraught. They knew that they wouldn't be able to conceal Liam's disappearance for very long. His flatmates must already be wondering where he was, and on Monday morning Mr Cleat would want to know what had happened to him. And then there was the question of Liam's car, still parked outside 93 Madeira Terrace.

"We'll have to visit some more of Mr Vane's

houses," said Lucy. "What we need is a map, with all of the special list properties marked on it."

"We'll only have time to look at two or three."

"That'll be enough. So long as we can find some more evidence. And next time we'll take it with us."

John said nervously, "What do you think's doing it? All this screaming and running and sucking people into the walls?"

"Nothing I've ever heard of before, and I used to read tonnes of horror books. I mean, it's not vampires, is it, no matter what Liam used to say about Mr Vane. I suppose it could be a poltergeist. You remember in that film when the little girl got caught inside the television? Poltergeists are supposed to make a lot of noise and throw things around."

"What about the statue?"

"John, I know it *looked* like the statue, but it couldn't have been. All you saw was a man with a very pale face. Your mind made the connection, and click, you thought it was him. Or *it*, rather."

John shrugged. He knew what he had seen, but he was too tired to carry on arguing any longer.

The next morning, Lucy told Mr Cleat that Liam had phoned her over the weekend to say that he wouldn't be coming into work for a day or two, on account of a bad summer cold.

"I suppose he didn't want to lose a sale by

sneezing all over the clients," said John, impressed by his own quickness. Mr Cleat gave him a pinched, intolerant look.

Before lunch, John had to go out with Courtney to show a young newly-married couple around a small maisonette backing on to the main London-Brighton railway line. When they got back, Lucy was waiting for him, but he couldn't go out with her immediately because Courtney wanted a cup of coffee and Mr Cleat wanted him to staple together a pile of particulars.

"Which house do you reckon we should look at next?" he asked Lucy, in the kitchen.

"This one is the closest ... 112 Abingdon Gardens, Tooting. If Cleaty wasn't here we could get the key."

At that moment, however, Mr Cleat came in and said, "John, I shall be out for half an hour. If anybody wants me, they can get me on my mobile."

"OK, Mr Cleat."

Lucy went to the front of the office to make sure that he had gone. Then she went straight into Mr Vane's room.

"Hey, what are you doing?" Courtney demanded. "Cleaty would have a fit if he saw you in there."

"We're going to take a look at another of Mr Vane's houses," said Lucy. John watched from the doorway as she went to Mr Vane's desk and tugged at the drawer handle.

"Locked," she said. "He's only gone and locked it."

"Perhaps he's guessed what we're up to," said John.

"This is out of order," Courtney protested. "I'm supposed to be the senior staff member here when Cleaty's away. I can't just let you ransack Mr Vane's office."

"John, get me a knife, would you? Maybe I can force this open."

"No," Courtney insisted. "I know you think that Mr Vane's up to something weird, but you can't break into his desk. Not when I'm in charge, anyway."

John looked at Lucy and he was sorely tempted to tell Courtney what had happened to Liam, but he knew that it wasn't the right time, not yet. Lucy said, "All right, then. If you don't want to help us, then don't. But we're still going to go and look at Mr Vane's houses."

"I don't know what you expect to find."

"More bones, that's what. More skeletons. And more evidence that Mr Vane knows exactly what happens when people go to live in his houses."

"I can't believe any of this. How could he have got away with killing all of those people? Don't tell me that nobody missed them."

"Of course people missed them. But if somebody disappears for ever and you never find out where they've gone, what can you do about it? Nothing. In the end, you can't help forgetting about them, can you?"

"But you're talking about *dozens* of people. Men, women and children. And just look at Mr Vane. He's as skinny as a rake. He wouldn't have the strength to step on an ant."

"You don't need to be strong to kill people," John put in. "All you need is a way to do it."

"Like what?"

Like a house that can suck you into its walls, thought John, but Lucy said, "We don't know exactly. That's what we're trying to find out."

"Well ... I don't know," said Courtney. "But all right, then. Go and take a look at the house if you want to. If Cleaty comes back, I'll tell him you're out with a client."

"You believe us?"

"I don't know. But I've always thought there was something fishy about Mr Vane and his special list, and even if he hasn't been murdering people I'd like to know what it is."

Abingdon Gardens was a quiet side street off the main Mitcham Road. While the rest of the area had been taken over by discount tyre companies and kebab restaurants and the pavements were cluttered with newspapers, Abingdon Gardens had retained most of its suburban gentility. The houses were large redbrick family properties screened from the road by laurel bushes, and almost all of them had names like "Windermere" and "Ivanhoe" and "The Laurels".

Number 112 was right at the very end, and much more neglected than any of the others. It had a *For Sale* sign outside, with the added instruction to "contact Mr Vane personally". The laurels were overgrown and weeds sprouted up between the red and white tiles of the path.

"Perhaps we shouldn't do this," said John. Now that they were actually here, he was beginning once again to feel that terrible sense of dread. Even on a warm summer day, this house had an atmosphere that was even more unwelcoming than 93 Madeira Terrace.

Lucy took a deep breath. He could see that she was just as frightened as he was. But she gave his hand a quick squeeze and said, "Come on. We have to. Nobody else is going to do it if we don't."

John climbed out of the car. He waited until Lucy had joined him and then he went across the weedy grass and peered into the garage window. It was very dark inside, but he could just make out the shape of a large car, draped in tarpaulin.

"Look at this," he said. "Who leaves their car behind when they move?"

"I don't know. What if they haven't moved?"

"You mean—"

"What if they're still in the house?"

"In the walls, you mean? Like Liam, and all those other people in Norbury?"

John stepped away from the garage and looked up at the house. "Perhaps we shouldn't do this," he repeated. But he knew that they had to.

They tried to see in through the living-room windows. "Looks empty," said Lucy.

John said, "We're going to have to tell somebody about Liam sooner or later."

"I know. But not yet. Not until we can prove what happened to him. And this is the only way we can prove it."

They made their way through long grass and brambles to the back garden. At the far end there was an overgrown strawberry bed and a tennis court with a sagging net. A stone Cupid had fallen on his side and a snail was leaving a silvery trail across his cheek. Most of the rear of the house was taken up by a conservatory. Inside they could see two or three frayed basketwork chairs and a row of earthenware pots containing black, shrivelled cacti.

John tried the conservatory door handle but it was locked. He stepped back into the garden and looked up at the first-floor windows. "Maybe I could try climbing up on to the conservatory roof and opening that small skylight."

"Too dangerous," said Lucy. "If you fell through that roof you could be killed."

"Then how are we going to get in?"

They were still thinking when John thought he saw one of the upstairs curtains moving. Then – for a terrible split-second – he thought he saw a white face looking down at them.

"There's somebody in there!" he said, pointing up at the bedroom. "I saw them! There's definitely somebody in there! Run!"

Without any hesitation, they ran back through the weeds until they reached the front garden. Lucy had scratched her arm and it was beaded with blood.

"I saw a face," John panted. "A really white, white face."

"Perhaps it's a squatter, or a tramp or something."

"I don't know. I didn't see it for long enough."

Lucy held a handkerchief over her scratch. "So what do we do now?"

"Forget about it. Go back to the office."

"No, come on. If it's only a squatter..."

"But supposing it isn't?"

"What else could it be?"

"I don't know," said John. But he kept thinking about the calm, ivory-faced statue, and the man in the dark suit who had followed them up towards Brighton station.

Lucy took out her car keys and turned back to the car. But then she said, "No. This is stupid. We've come this far. We owe it to Liam."

"Lucy, I don't want to go in there."

"Well, I don't, either. But we could try ringing the doorbell first. Perhaps your white-faced man will come downstairs and answer it."

John didn't say anything. He knew that Lucy was talking sense, but his reluctance to go back to the house was so strong that he didn't even know if his legs would take him up to the front door.

"Come on," said Lucy, and together they walked up to the porch, although John kept his eyes on the first-floor windows. They remained empty, like the eyes of somebody who has forgotten their reason for living.

John reached out at arm's length and pressed the doorbell. They could hear the bell ringing somewhere in the house. They waited for a while, and then John rang again, and again. Still no reply. Still no sign of life.

"Perhaps you didn't see what you thought you saw," Lucy suggested.

"It was a face, I'm sure of it."

"Well, let's go round to the back and have another try. I don't think there's anybody here."

They returned to the back garden and John pointed up to the window. "It was there. Only for a second."

Lucy moved her head from side to side. "There *is* something. But I think it's just a reflection. There must be a dressing-table mirror in there, or something like that. Look, it's oval-shaped. You could easily mistake it for a face."

"I'm sure the curtain moved, too."

"Oh, come on. We've both got the jitters, that's all."

John shaded his eyes and looked up at it again. Lucy could be right. And after all, there was no sign at all that anybody was living here.

"The key's inside the conservatory door, still in the lock," said Lucy. "I vote we break the glass."

"That's breaking and entering."

"No, it's not. It's an estate agent's security check. We just happened to be passing one of our company's properties and thought we saw an intruder. We broke in to make sure that our property wasn't being used by squatters."

John suddenly remembered that Liam had come up with a similar excuse for breaking into 93 Madeira Terrace, and he felt a shiver of foreboding, as if they were repeating the opening lines of a play that always ended in the same horrific way.

Lucy dislodged a brick from the edge of the patio and handed it to him. Underneath, the brick was crawling with woodlice, and he had to knock it against the step to get them off.

Oh God, he thought. *What if I break the window and the white-faced man comes after me? What if we get into the house and he traps us inside? What if—*

"*Hurry up!*" hissed Lucy.

Cautiously, John went up to the conservatory door. It was divided into six glass panels so at least he wouldn't have to smash it all. "Go on," Lucy urged him. "Go on before anybody sees us."

John hesitated for a few moments more. Then he swung back his arm and hit the window as hard as he could. It shattered with an ear-splitting crack that he was sure could be heard three miles away, and the glass fell to the conservatory floor like a carillon of sleigh-bells.

They waited to see if anybody had heard them, but the suburban noises went on just as before: children screaming in a playground, lawnmowers, the rattle of a distant train. John reached inside and turned the key and the conservatory door opened with a shudder.

They crossed the conservatory and tried the double doors that led to the sitting-room. "Locked again," said John, rattling the door handles. Without a word, Lucy handed him the brick, and this time, he smashed the window with no hesitation at all.

The sitting-room was furnished with a huge, shapeless three-piece suite covered with dust-sheets. There was a brown tiled fireplace with a coal-effect electric fire, a tall mahogany standard-lamp with a mock-parchment shade and a magazine rack still stuffed with yellowing copies of the *Radio Times*.

One of the chairs must still have had some lumpy cushions on it, because it looked to John as if somebody was sitting in it, utterly motionless, concealed beneath the dust sheet. He watched it out of the corner of his eye as he walked across the room, in case he saw it move in and out to the rhythm of somebody's breathing.

He ventured into the dining-room while Lucy went into the kitchen. There was a hefty 1930s dining-table and a huge maple-veneered sideboard with a dusty octagonal mirror hanging above it. In the window stood a faded display of dried flowers and bracken.

"Anything?" he called out to Lucy.

"Not in the kitchen. But there's tins of peas and carrots in the larder, and a loaf of bread in the bread-bin that's practically turned to stone."

John opened the drawer in the top of the sideboard. Inside, tarnished silver cutlery lay like a shoal of goldfish. Whoever had lived here had left almost everything behind. It was as if they had just walked out of their life and never returned.

As he closed the drawer, he thought he could see a reflection in the mirror of a dark, pale-faced figure standing in the hallway behind him. He was so frightened that he felt as if cold fingers were running down his back. He didn't even dare to turn around. Instead, he reached up with a trembling hand and wiped the dust from the mirror so that he could see the apparition more clearly.

When he did so, however, it disappeared, and Lucy came in through the door as if there was nothing there at all.

"What's the matter?" she asked him.

"I saw it again. The statue."

"Where?" she said, looking nervously around. "I didn't see anything."

John pushed past her and went out in the hallway. He looked left and right, and then he looked upstairs. A weak light filtered through net curtains the colour of cold tea. "I saw it. I swear I did."

"John, that statue was solid wood. It weighed a tonne. Nobody could carry it around even if they wanted to."

"That's the point. It wasn't being carried around. It was alive."

"*Alive?*"

"I saw it standing behind me. I swear it."

Lucy said, "Enough, John. You're really letting this get to you." But he could tell that – for all her reassurance – she was just as scared as he was.

"I swear to you I saw it. It was right there, standing in the hallway."

"Perhaps you're right. Perhaps we'd better go."

John said, "Wait." A sudden thought had occurred to him and he went back into the sitting-room. The chairs were all still covered by their dust sheets, and the lumpy one apparently undisturbed. Yet where else could the figure have gone so quickly?

John approached the chair with his heart beating hard.

"You don't think it's under *there?*" asked Lucy.

John was too frightened even to answer her. He bent down and took hold of the trailing edge of the dust sheet. He lifted it up a little way, and then he gave it a sharp sideways tug. Lucy squealed in terror, and John jumped back, stumbling against the arm of the sofa.

In the chair were two braided cushions, a rolled-up mat and an anglepoise desk lamp. Lucy pressed her hand over her heart in relief.

"Let's take a very quick look upstairs," she said. "Then I think we'd better get out of here."

John's instinct was to leave there and then, but he followed Lucy to the bottom of the stairs. They both looked up to the landing. On the walls were six or seven small landscape paintings, all of them depicting deserted heathland or rainswept mountains.

There was something infinitely depressing about these pictures, and John noticed that in each of them there was a small group of figures dressed in cloaks, like monks, and in some of them there was a tall dark figure with horns.

"Don't you just hate these pictures?" said Lucy, as she followed John up the stairs.

The stairs didn't creak, but John stopped halfway up to listen.

"Did you hear something?" he asked.

"An aeroplane, that's all."

"No, it wasn't that. It was something like a really heavy blanket being *dragged*."

Lucy listened, wide-eyed. "No ... I didn't hear anything."

John listened for a moment longer and then continued upstairs. They reached the landing and looked around. All of the bedroom doors were closed, and there was the dead, warm and airless smell of a closed-up house in summer.

John opened the first door on the right. It swung back silently and swiftly, almost as if somebody were opening it from the inside. The room was in semi-darkness because the curtains were drawn. It was wallpapered with florid pink flowers. He could see the end of a bed covered in a brown candlewick bedspread, and an upright wooden chair. "Nothing," he said, and he was just about to close the door again when Lucy pointed and whispered, "*Look*."

"What?" he said. "I can't see anything."

"Down by the bedside table. *There*."

John frowned into the gloom and then he saw what Lucy was pointing at. At first he had thought it was just another flower on the wallpaper, but as his eyes focused he saw what it really was.

A human skull, half-buried in the wall, its eye-sockets revealing nothing but wallpaper, its mouth stretched wide as if it were screaming at them.

11

John pushed the door open a little wider and stepped into the room. He bent down a respectful distance from the skull and peered at it intently. "That's horrible. It's not very big, is it? It must be a woman or a child."

"This looks like a child's bedroom, doesn't it?" said Lucy. "A little girl's probably. Oh God, do you think that could be *her*?"

"This is the proof we've been looking for," said John. "I bet all of the properties on Mr Vane's special list are the same. People come to live in them and the houses suck them in."

"Yes, but who would want to come and live here? Not with something like *this* in the wall."

John felt very grim. "Don't worry," he told her.

"I expect Mr Vane gives his properties the once-over before he shows anybody around. But I wonder why this skull is sticking out like this?"

Lucy said, "That poor little girl. I hope she didn't suffer."

John thought of Liam's last desperate appeal for help as he was sucked into the wall, but said nothing.

Lucy knelt down close to the skull. Then she suddenly said, "Look at this. Look what she's got round her neck."

John came closer. Now he could see that looped around the base of the skull was a small silver crucifix on a silver chain. The wall had taken her in as far as that but no further.

They heard more noises. A creak, and then a sound like a door being very carefully closed. "We'd better go now," said Lucy. "We've got to think what we're going to do next."

"Call the police, of course, as soon as we can. But let's make sure that we stay around here until they come. We don't want the evidence destroyed this time."

They left the bedroom. Lucy locked the door and dropped the key into John's coat pocket.

They reached the top of the stairs and were just starting to go down them when John heard the dragging noise again. He stopped, and gripped Lucy's shoulder. "There – you must have heard it that time."

"I don't know. It sounded like—"

She stopped, with her mouth open. Around the corner in the corridor appeared the tall, dark figure with its pale ivory face. But even though it still had the same frightening calmness, it was no longer the lifeless wooden statue that John had found on the bed. It moved towards them gracefully and swiftly, almost *gliding* rather than walking, its eyes unblinking, its face handsome and serene. As it moved, it was accompanied by the soft dragging noise that they had heard before: its cloak-hem, sweeping the floor.

For a long, long second, John didn't know how to move his arms or legs. Then Lucy made a peculiar noise, a kind of choked-up whimper of absolute fear, and the two of them hurtled down the stairs as fast as they could. Behind them they heard soft, leaping footsteps, as if the statue were coming down the stairs four and five at a time.

"*Open the door! Open the door!*" Lucy squealed, as John struggled with the unfamiliar lock. He managed to open it, but the door jarred on a safety chain and he had to shut it again so that he could slide the chain free. At that moment the statue caught hold of him and threw him against the door. John dropped to the floor, stunned and winded.

Lucy managed to wrestle open the door but the statue seized it and banged it shut. Lucy screamed and tried to dodge out of its way, but it caught hold of her wrist and held her tight, staring into her face with the same terrible lack of emotion. John managed to drag himself on to his feet, coughing and whining for breath. He lifted the heavy walking-stick out of the umbrella-stand, gripped it in both hands and struck the statue across the side of the head. The walking-stick snapped in half, but the statue released Lucy's wrist and turned back to John.

"*Run!*" John shouted, and Lucy ran – through the sitting-room and into the conservatory. John tried to duck and feint his way around the statue, but the figure was much too quick for him. It never blinked and it seemed to be able to anticipate every move he made.

It glided nearer and nearer, one hand raised as if it intended to take him by the throat. John backed into the corner and tripped against the umbrella stand.

"*John!*" shrilled Lucy, and as she did so, one of the earthenware cactus pots came flying through the air and hit the statue right in the back, exploding into fragments. The statue turned its head, and as it did so John rolled across the floor, staggered on to his feet, and ran after Lucy as if all the demons in hell were after him.

They sprinted through the weeds to the front of the house. Brambles snatched against John's shirtsleeves as if they were trying to catch him.

They ran out of the front gate and jumped into Lucy's car, and they were halfway down Abingdon Gardens before the pale-faced figure appeared outside the house, watching them drive away.

"I told you," John gasped. There was a wide crimson bruise on his left cheekbone. "I *told* you it was there."

"Well, you didn't expect me to *believe* you, did you? Statues can't come to life."

"This one has. And not only that, it was waiting for us. It was waiting for us in Brighton and it was waiting for us here."

"It couldn't have been," said Lucy. "No one knew that we were coming here, only us."

"It couldn't have been a coincidence, though, could it?"

"How should I know? This whole thing is scaring me to death." Lucy was so upset that she could hardly drive straight, and when they reached the Mitcham Road junction she changed gear with a hideous grinding noise.

"Do you think Mr Vane has guessed what we're doing?" asked John.

"I don't see how. Not unless Courtney's told him, and Courtney wouldn't tell."

"Well – I know this sounds mad – but if the statue can come to life, perhaps the statue told him."

"*What?*"

"We found the statue when we broke into 66 Mountjoy Avenue, didn't we? It looked as if it was made of wood, but perhaps it could still see us and hear us."

"But if Mr Vane knows what we're doing, why doesn't he just warn us off, or sack us?"

"I'm not sure. Perhaps it's too late for that. We've found out too much already. I think he wants to get rid of us completely. You know –" and he drew his finger across his throat.

"In that case, it's definitely time to call the police."

"I don't know. I'm not so sure any more. If Mr Vane knows what we're doing, he's going to make sure that he gets rid of all the evidence, isn't he? And what kind of people do you think the police are going to think we are if we tell them that we're being hunted down by a wooden statue? That's right, nutters."

"Then what can we do? We can't go back to the office."

"Of course we can. Mr Vane can't murder us in broad daylight, can he? And if he openly warns us to stay away from the houses on his special list, that's an admission that he knows we've been to see them, and why." He gave a last look back along Abingdon Gardens. "No – we don't have to be frightened of going back to the office. What we have to watch out for is that statue."

Lucy said, "I still can't understand how it came to life – how it was waiting for us. It's so scary I don't even want to think about it."

Back in the office Mr Cleat was in a strange, agitated mood. As soon as John and Lucy walked in he said, "Ah!" and beckoned them over to his desk.

"Something wrong?" asked Lucy.

"Not exactly," said Mr Cleat. "But Mr Vane has expressed some concern about the increasing amount of time that some of you are spending out of the office without a corresponding rise in property sales."

"We can't *force* people to buy houses," Lucy protested.

"Obviously not. But Mr Vane wants to make sure that you keep your mind on what you're doing."

John glanced at Lucy. If that wasn't a veiled warning for them to keep away from Mr Vane's special list houses, he didn't know what was.

That evening they had to stay late to finish their weekly rearrangement of the houses in the office window, so Lucy asked John if he'd like to go for a drink at The Feathers across the road, where Courtney was already waiting. She reached out for his hand as they crossed the road and he grasped it firmly as he helped her through the traffic. She couldn't stand men with damp or floppy hands, she had told him. Shaking hands with Cleaty was like fondling a fillet of haddock.

Courtney was at the bar, talking to two rival estate agents – a man with a clipped moustache and a clipped accent to go with it, and a woman in a violent red dress who smoked incessantly and smelled as if she had tipped a whole bottle of perfume over herself.

Courtney made his excuses and led John and Lucy over to a corner table. It was early, so the pub wasn't too crowded, and there was nobody near to overhear what they were saying.

"So what happened at Abingdon Gardens?" asked Courtney. "Is that where you got those bruises?"

John nodded. "I know this is going to sound as if we're bonkers, but I swear it's the truth." He told Courtney everthing that had happened at Mountjoy Avenue and at Abingdon Gardens that morning. At first Courtney started to smile and shake his head, especially when John told them about the statue, but Lucy reached out and touched his hand and gave him a look which meant *it really happened, all of it*.

Courtney said, "I'll tell you something, this is all very hard to believe. No wonder you haven't told the police."

"It's true, Courtney," said Lucy. "On my life, it's all absolutely true."

"Do you think you're going to be safe? I mean, if Mr Vane's got this statue-thing coming after you..."

"We don't really have any proof that Mr Vane sent it. But so far we've only seen it when we've been visiting Mr Vane's houses. It could be a kind of guardian, you know. A watchdog. Something he uses to keep away unwelcome visitors."

"Oh, come on," said Courtney. "It has to be a guy in fancy dress."

Lucy emphatically shook her head. "You wouldn't say that if you saw it."

"So how does it know where to find you? And how does it get from house to house? Unless there are more than one of them."

Lucy shrugged. "We really don't know. I'm not sure that we really want to find out. But I think we're going to have to."

"Why?" asked Courtney. "Can't you just give Mr Vane's houses a very wide berth? The police are investigating all those old bones in the Norbury house and the odds must be that they'll find *some* way of connecting them to Mr Vane."

"It's more personal than old bones," said Lucy. "Go on, tell him, John." And John, with his eyes fixed on the table, one hand endlessly rotating a beer mat, told Courtney all about Liam. By the time he had finished they were all in tears.

"I have to go away and think about this," said Courtney. "This has come as such a shock."

"I just didn't know what to do," John told him.

Courtney said, "You should have come to me before. If the three of us go to the police they're bound to believe us. They're bound to look into it, anyway."

"But what if they can't find anything?"

"Forget it, John. This isn't something we can handle on our own. Let's sleep on it tonight. Then we can have a meeting in the office in the morning and decide what we're going to say to the CID."

"All right," John agreed, and gave Lucy's hand another non-damp, non-floppy squeeze.

It was dark by the time they left the pub. Lucy said, "Come on, John, I'll give you a lift. It'll take you ages to get home on the bus."

They drove southwards through the crowded evening traffic. "Are you glad we told Courtney?" Lucy asked him.

John said, "Yes. But I'm still worried that Mr Vane's going to get away with it. When you think of all the people who must have gone missing over the years – all of them sucked into those houses – and yet there's Mr Vane walking around free, a respected member of the community."

They turned into John's street and drove towards his house. His father's old B-reg Morris Marina was parked outside under the streetlight. "Just stop behind it," said John, unfastening his seat-belt and preparing to get out.

"Hold on a minute," said Lucy, as she switched off the engine. "There's somebody standing outside your house."

John looked up and frowned. He hadn't noticed until now that there was a tall, dark figure waiting in the shadow of their privet hedge.

"I wasn't *expecting* anybody," said John.

But then the figure took one step forward out of the shadows and he saw who it was. Or rather, *what* it was.

"*Go!*" he shouted to Lucy, slamming the car door shut. "*Go!* It's him! He's been waiting for us!"

Lucy twisted the key in the ignition and the starter–motor whinnied and whinnied but at last it caught. She tugged the gearstick into reverse and skidded away backwards, just as the statue pummelled the bonnet of her car with its fists.

"*Faster!*" John yelled at her, and the Metro snaked wildly down the road with its transmission whining. Lucy tried to turn the car around so that she could drive away forwards, but as she did so she collided with a parked van, which jolted John so hard that he knocked his head against the window. Lucy wrestled the gearstick into first, but when she tried to drive away the tyres spun on the roadway with an acrid smell of burned rubber and they didn't move at all.

John twisted around in his seat. "Your bumper's locked!" he yelled at her. Only metres away, the statue was coming towards them with one arm lifted, its face expressionless.

John opened his door and hurried around to the back of the car. The Metro's rear bumper was caught beneath the van's front wing. He tried kicking it free but he couldn't dislodge it. He looked up and the statue had almost reached them.

"When I say 'hit it!' – put your foot down!" John shouted.

The statue came remorselessly up to the car. Out of its cloak it drew a long knob-ended stick. It swung the stick around, and smashed the front headlight. Then it swung again and the windscreen burst inwards, showering Lucy in glass. John spread his hands flat on the car's roof, jumped up as high as he could, and shouted, "*Hit it!*"

Lucy revved the engine and let out the clutch, just as John landed on the rear bumper with both feet. The Metro surged forward with John clinging to the back of it. As it sped away, the statue swept its stick around in one last desperate attempt to catch them, and hit John a blow on the shoulder that almost knocked him into the road.

Lucy stopped and John scrambled back into his seat.

"What do we do now?" he panted, as she pressed down hard on the accelerator and they roared away.

"We can stay at my uncle Robin's house. Mr Vane doesn't know where *he* lives. I'll just have to go back to my flat and get a change of clothes."

John twisted around in his seat but he couldn't see the statue any more. "How did it find out where I live?" he wanted to know. "And how did it get here?"

"I don't know how it got here, but think about it: Mr Vane knows where you live, doesn't he? I think this is proof that he knows about the statue and if he knows about the statue he probably knows about the skeletons, too."

"I hope the statue doesn't hurt my mum and dad, that's all."

"When we get back to my place, you can ring them, can't you?"

"Yes," said John, worriedly. As they drove back through Streatham, his shoulder began to throb and he realized how hard the statue had hit him.

They reached a small parade of shops opposite Tooting Graveney Common, and parked outside a greengrocers'. "My flat's upstairs," said Lucy. "Come on, I won't be long, and you can give your parents a quick call. But I think it had better be quick. Mr Vane knows were *I* live, too."

She took out her key and unlocked the door. John waited while she picked up a scattering of post and pressed the time-switch to turn on the lights. A ridiculously steep flight of stairs led directly up to the first-floor landing. John followed her up, still nursing his shoulder.

They were only halfway up when the lights abruptly went out, leaving them in total darkness.

"Stupid time-switch. Can you feel your way up?"

"Yeah, I think so."

They carried on climbing the stairs, sliding their hands up the handrail to guide them. "It's the landlady, she's so mean she only gives you about three seconds to get to your flat. I'm surprised that nobody's been killed, falling down these stairs."

John heard Lucy reach the top. "Switch is here somewhere," she said, groping against the wall. "Hang on, it's next to this picture."

The lights popped on again. As they did so, John blinked and saw a narrow corridor with a single low-watt light-bulb dangling from the ceiling. It was hardly enough to illuminate the doorway at the very end of the corridor. But it was just enough to shine on the chilling white face which was waiting for them in the shadows.

12

John snatched Lucy's sleeve and without a word the two of them hurtled back down towards the front door. But the stairs were so steep that Lucy lost her footing halfway down. She collided into John, and then the two of them tumbled the last six or seven stairs until they landed in a tangle in the hallway.

"*Get up!*" John screamed, trying to pull Lucy to her feet.

He looked up the stairs and the statue was gliding down towards them, almost as if it were floating a few centimetres above the treads. One of its hands was resting lightly on the handrail, and John would never forget the sound that it made – a hollow, descending hiss, like the softest of slide-whistles.

He managed to haul Lucy up, but immediately she cried out and collapsed again. "My ankle! I've twisted my ankle!"

"Hold on to me!" John told her, and wrapped her left arm around his shoulders. Together they staggered to the front door, just as the statue reached the foot of the stairs. Lucy opened the door and they hop-hobbled out on to the pavement and across to Lucy's car.

"I can't drive! My ankle hurts too much!"

"Give me the keys, then!"

John opened the car door and lifted Lucy into the passenger seat. He ran around to the driver's side and threw himself behind the wheel. The statue had almost reached them, and as he started the engine it beat on the roof of the car so loudly that Lucy shrieked and covered her ears.

They drove away from the kerb in a series of wild jerks, and when John changed into second it sounded as if he were tearing the gearbox into small jagged pieces.

"Have you passed your test?" Lucy shouted at him.

"Not yet. I'm going to take it when I've had some lessons."

"What? You've never had any lessons?"

He changed quite smoothly into third. "Don't worry about it. I know how to drive. My dad taught me when we were on holiday."

The wind whistled in through the shattered windscreen and Lucy looked around at her car. The statue had dented the roof in so deeply that it almost touched their heads. The bonnet looked like a West Indian steel drum and only one of the headlights was intact. "Oh, well," she said, "I don't suppose a few more scratches will make any difference."

John glanced in the rearview mirror. "I think we've lost it again."

"It *must* have been sent by Mr Vane, if it knows where I live, too."

"What I want to know is, unless there's more than one statue, how did it get to your place so fast? And your door was locked. How did it manage to get in?"

Lucy winced as she tried to find a comfortable place to rest her ankle. "I don't know, John. But it's not going to stop until it gets us, is it?"

John reached Streatham High Road and stopped. "Where do we go now?" he asked her.

"Uncle Robin's. He lives on Mitcham Common."

"Who's Uncle Robin?"

"My dad's older brother. Very much older brother. He was the only child of my grandfather's first marriage."

A car had been waiting behind them and it gave John an impatient toot. "Come on," said Lucy, "turn left and head for Mitcham. I'll direct you."

John found driving much harder than he had thought it would be. How could drivers look so relaxed when they had to steer and change gear and make signals *and* look where they were going, all at the same time? When he turned into Greyhound Lane he drove over the nearside kerb and almost collided with a bollard. His teeth were clenched with concentration and salt perspiration stung his eyes.

"Dear God, I hope that thing can't follow us," said Lucy.

To John's relief, they arrived at last outside a small end-of-terrace house facing the scrubby heathland of Mitcham Common. He helped Lucy out of the car and up the path. The front garden was concreted over and populated by small conversational groups of concrete gnomes and concrete rabbits.

Lucy rang the door chimes and they played the first bars of *The White Cliffs of Dover*. The door was opened by a small bespectacled man with a large bald dome surrounded by a halo of fine white hair. He had protuberant blue eyes and a nose that looked as if he had bought it in a joke shop.

"Goodness me, if it isn't Lucy! What are you doing here?"

"It's a surprise," said Lucy, trying to sound cheerful.

"Why didn't you ring to tell me you were

coming? I could have bought you some Battenberg cake."

"Uncle Robin, I haven't eaten Battenberg cake since I was six."

Lucy managed to hop into the hallway and John followed her. The house was very small and smelled of pipe tobacco and meat pie.

"What have you done to your ankle, young lady?"

"I've had a bit of a crash in the car. This is John, from work. He was very kind and drove me here."

"Come and sit down. Here – put this pouffe under your ankle. You haven't hurt yourself anywhere else, have you? Haven't got whiplash?"

He helped Lucy to make herself comfortable and then he said, "How about a cup of tea? Nothing like a cup of tea after a nasty turn. What about you, John?"

"No, no thanks," said John. He looked around at the sitting-room. The mantelpiece was cluttered with pipes and half-dismantled clocks and family photographs and all kinds of assorted junk. But there were six or seven framed diplomas on the wall, showing that Uncle Robin was a doctor of anthropology and a winner of the Blackwell history prize and all kinds of other awards.

"Perhaps you'd like to ring your mum and dad – let them know where you are."

"No thanks, Uncle Robin. I don't want to worry them."

"They'll want you to spend a few days at home, won't they? You won't be walking on that ankle for a bit."

"Actually, I was wondering if John and I could stay here for a couple of days."

"Here?" Uncle Robin frowned at Lucy and then at John. "Why would you want to stay here? I mean, you're very welcome. But you're not in some kind of trouble, are you?"

"Actually, yes," said John. "Lucy and I got mixed up in something at work. Now we've got some people looking for us and we don't want them to know where we are."

Uncle Robin took a deep breath. "I don't suppose you want to tell me what this 'something' is that you've got mixed up in?"

"It's very complicated," said Lucy. "It's all to do with property deals."

"It sounds as if you've found out about something you shouldn't have."

"Yes ... you could say that."

"Then without knowing any of the details, I really think your best answer is to go to the police. There are some pretty nasty types around this area."

"We can't go yet," said John. "We don't have enough proof. But when we do..."

"Do you need any help – apart from somewhere to stay?"

"No, thanks. We're fine for the moment."

"And you really don't want to tell me what this 'something' is all about?"

"If you don't mind – if you don't think we're being too rude..."

"All right," said Uncle Robin, raising his hands in mock-surrender. "If you don't want to tell me, I really don't mind."

Uncle Robin poured out tea while John telephoned his father. "It's all right, Dad. I'm staying with a friend tonight. I'll see you tomorrow."

"You could have rung me before I put the chicken in the oven, couldn't you? That's the trouble with you, you never think."

"No, Dad. Sorry, Dad."

"Your mother says what are you going to do for clean underpants?"

John was put up in a small room at the back under the eaves. The sheets were cold and unfamiliar and there were no curtains at the window so that the moon shone in and illuminated an ironing-board and a chair with a huge grimy doll in it, her enamelled face affected on one side by a kind of leprosy.

He heard Lucy hobble to the bathroom and then hobble back to her bedroom. Probably taking another paracetamol to dull the pain of her twisted ankle. He heard Uncle Robin come creaking up the stairs and flush the toilet. Then the house fell silent and he lay awake wishing that he had never meddled in Mr Vane's affairs, and feeling so guilty about Liam that it gave him a physical pain in his stomach.

Next morning they phoned Courtney at the office and told him what had happened.

"That's it, I'm going to call the police," said Courtney.

"Courtney, please. Not yet. They won't believe a word of it."

"Come on, man. What more evidence do you need?"

"We need proof that Mr Vane knew what his houses would do to people before he put them on the market – but that he still sold them, regardless. It's almost like he was *feeding* his houses, do you know what I mean?"

"And this statue-thing that's chasing you, what about that? What if it catches up with you? What if it kills you?"

John said, "As far as we can guess, Mr Vane is sending it after us. Well, either him or Cleaty, and I don't think Cleaty's got anything to do with all this. If we can't produce enough evidence to have Mr Vane arrested and put away, then that statue's going to keep on coming after us and it's never going to let us go."

There was a long pause. Then Courtney said, "All right, then. I won't tell the police just yet. But tell me if there's anything else I can do to help you."

Lucy took the phone. "There is – if you can manage it. See if you can open up Mr Vane's desk and get copies of his keys. Then we'll be able to visit more of his houses – all of them, if we have to. All we need is one piece of really concrete evidence."

"I don't know," said Courtney. "Supposing I get caught? I don't want to sound like a coward or anything, but I don't want that statue coming after *me*, no way."

"So you really do believe us."

"I don't think I have any choice, do I? Either you're stark-staring mad, the both of you, or else you're telling me the truth."

"Has Cleaty said anything about us not showing up for work?"

"I told him you'd both caught Liam's cold. I don't think he believed me but he didn't seem to care. He's been acting very strangely. He keeps leaving the office for hours on end and coming back all peculiar, like he's got something on his mind."

"What about Mr Vane?"

"No sign of him at all."

"Thanks, Courtney. We'll call you later. And do try to get hold of those keys."

They spent the morning with a map of the British Isles spread out on Uncle Robin's dining table, covered with a sheet of tracing paper. Using John's copy of the special list, they pinpointed every one of Mr Vane's properties, twenty-seven of them altogether. Then they sat back and stared at the map they had drawn and tried to make sense out of it.

"Maybe there's no logic in it at all," said John, drinking tea. "Maybe some houses are haunted and some aren't, and that's all there is to it."

Uncle Robin came in, sucking on a pipe that wouldn't light. He leaned over their map and studied it for a very long time without saying anything.

"What do these crosses represent?" he asked them, at last.

"Houses. We've been trying to work out some connection between them. The trouble is, there just doesn't seem to be any. Some of them are old, some of them are new. And they're scattered all over the place."

Uncle Robin ran his finger north-westwards up the map, through a number of the crosses, until it reached Derbyshire. "Not exactly *scattered*," he said.

"What do you mean?" asked John, getting out of his chair and standing beside him.

"Well, look. If you were to draw a line from this

house here in Salisbury to this house here in Bromsgrove, up near Birmingham, and then on to this house in Congleton, what would you get?"

John was perplexed, but Uncle Robin picked up a newspaper and used the edge of it like a ruler.

"Yeah, I see what you mean," said John. "A completely straight line."

"That's right. And that's unusual enough, in itself. But this isn't any old completely straight line, is it? Look where else this line runs through." With the tip of his tobacco-stained forefinger, he slowly retraced its route through the English shires.

"It runs through Stonehenge," said John.

"That's it ... you've twigged it. And not just Stonehenge, but look here – this Iron Age fort at Old Sarum, and Salisbury Cathedral, and this Iron Age camp at Clearbury Ring, and this Iron Age hill fort at Frankenbury Camp. All of your houses exactly line up with three-thousand-year-old ancient monuments."

Lucy limped up and stared at the map, too. "And?" she wanted to know.

"And there's only one explanation. This line is the Old Sarum Ley."

"I don't get it," said John. "What's the Old Sarum Ley?"

"It's one of Britain's main ley lines, that's what."

John turned to Lucy but all Lucy could do was shrug.

Uncle Robin said, "Ley lines are straight, unwavering lines that run from one ancient site to another, from one side of the country to the other. Mathematically straight. They're still a mystery, as far as scientists are concerned, because the only way those monuments could have been aligned so accurately would have been by very advanced geometry and a knowledge of astronomy which people simply didn't possess in those days. We're talking about 900 BC, even earlier."

He peered at the map even more intently. Then he said, "Fetch me that T-square." John passed it to him, and he began to draw criss-cross lines all across their map.

"There," he said. "I don't know what you've got yourselves into, but here's your answer."

"The answer to what, Uncle?"

"The answer to what you've been drawing on your map. Every one of these houses falls exactly on an ancient ley line. Now, I don't know what trouble you've been in, and I know that I've promised not to ask, but not a single one of these houses was built on any of these sites by accident."

"You're *sure* about that?" John asked him.

"Of course I'm sure, lad, I wrote a book about it. *The Way of the Druids*. Awen Press, 1962. I've got a copy here somewhere if you want to take a look."

"So what *are* ley lines?" asked Lucy.

"They're supposed to be lines of incredible

magical force, running through the earth's crust. They're like a kind of primitive Internet, if you like, because they were supposed to be capable of carrying messages and warnings – and some scholars say that they were even capable of carrying solid objects, like stones, or daggers, or magical talismans – right from one side of the country to the other. The legend is that the stones from Stonehenge were carried through the earth along ley lines."

"But those stones weigh tonnes and tonnes."

"That's right, they do. But some experts say that goes to show just how powerful the ley lines are. They were supposed to have been there since the earth was first created, but it was the Druids who discovered them first, about 1000 BC."

"Oh, right. The Druids. We did them in school. They worshipped mistletoe, didn't they?"

"The Druids were a religious caste in ancient Britain – and, yes, you're right, they did worship mistletoe, and everything else that came from the oak tree. In fact, they believed that oak trees could actually speak, because they had spirits in them."

Lucy looked across at John and it was clear from the wide-eyed expression on her face that she was thinking about the statue.

Uncle Robin caught her look but he misinterpreted it. "You're entitled to have your doubts. But it's only fair to the Druids to say that when Julius Caesar invaded Britain and first came across them, he was deeply impressed by what they knew about the earth and the stars, and what he called 'the nature of things and the power and prerogatives of the immortal gods'.

"The Druids practised medicine and sorcery, and they believed that when they died their souls would live for ever. They killed people so that they could feed on their spiritual strength. They believed that even after death, when their bodies had rotted away, their spirits would continue to live within the earth, and within the trees; and that they would still go on taking human sacrifices for ever, dragging people into the netherworld."

"That's scary," said Lucy.

"Yes, you're quite right. It's *very* scary. But they also believed that men were capable of anything, provided that they remained in close contact with Awen, the divine name, and the eye of the light, which is the sun shining through a specially-built collection of upright stones – like Stonehenge, for instance."

John sat down and stared at the map. "The trouble is – even if all of these houses *are* built on ley lines, what does it mean? And, you know, what does it *prove*?"

"Don't ask me. I've just given you the answer, but so far you haven't even told me what the question is."

"The question is, why do you think these houses are all built along ley lines?"

Uncle Robin made another unsuccessful attempt to light his pipe. "Let me tell you one thing – they wouldn't have been built there for the benefit of the occupants. Living on a ley line is rather like living on the San Andreas Fault in America, only much more frightening. An earthquake is only an earthquake, after all. You might get hit on the head by a large chunk of falling masonry. Your house might collapse. But at least an earthquake doesn't walk casually into the room and take your *soul*."

"What? What are you talking about, your *soul*?"

Uncle Robin said, "I think I've said too much already."

"Tell us," John demanded.

"All right, so long as you promise to keep an open mind. *I* believe in the power of ley lines but a lot of people don't. A lot of it is nothing but legend, after all. Fantasy. Stories passed down from mother to daughter, for hundreds and hundreds of years. The Druids gradually died out, but they had themselves buried along ley lines so that even after death their spirits would still be able to travel."

"Why would the Druids want to travel around the country so much?" asked Lucy.

"Because they're still all-powerful, as far as they're concerned, even though they've been dead for two thousand years. They still think that they own this country. They still think that they control its destiny. They're still sliding along those ley lines, like spiders sliding along their webs, sliding from north to south, from east to west. And God help you if you're young and vulnerable, and just happen to be standing on top of one of those ley lines when a Druid sweeps past, underneath you.

"You know those old children's warnings about not stepping on the cracks in the pavement, because bears would come up and get you? Those warnings weren't just a game, they were serious. But it wasn't bears that children had to be afraid of. It was the Ancient Order of Druids – and, believe you me, it still is."

"So they're actually underground?" asked Lucy.

Uncle Robin shook his head. "Not underground as such. They don't have any material substance themselves, not any more, so they exist in anything solid. Walls, doors, chairs, ceilings. If I thought that I was living anywhere near a ley line, I'd throw out my wardrobe. You could get eleven Druids in it, complete with sacrifical white bulls and golden sickles and all."

John said, "I still don't understand the houses."

"Well, I can't tell you for certain," said Uncle Robin. "But I suppose that travelling along ley lines must be a bit like travelling by submarine. Now and again you want to come up to the surface and stretch your legs and take on supplies. My guess is that these houses were built as places where Druid spirits could rest and recuperate and get their strength up."

"And *feed*?" said Lucy, her voice slightly wobbly.

"Well, of course, yes, feed."

Lucy's ankle buckled again and she had to sit down. John knelt beside her and took hold of her hand. Her uncle Robin bent down close and his face was very serious.

"What have you found, you two? I think you'd better tell me now."

13

They told him everything – about Mr Rogers, about Liam, and most of all about the statue. He listened to them without interrupting, and when they had finished he still remained silent for almost another two or three minutes, thinking.

"This is almost unbelievable. But I don't have any doubt at all that you've come across the greatest surviving network of pre-Christian magic that's ever been recorded."

"Do you mean people have found them before?"

"At least twice, so far as I know. You know Mont St Michel, in France – that monastery that's built on a rock and stands in the middle of the sea? That used to be a Druid place of worship before the Romans came.

"The actual monastery was finished about AD 1120 but part of it was burned down in 1203. When the builders came to repair it in 1211, they found the skeletons of more than twenty monks and pilgrims bricked up inside the foundations. Some of the skeletons were actually half-buried in the walls – just like that little girl's skull you found in Tooting.

"There was only one explanation. The spirits of the Druids were still there, after more than a thousand years, deep in the granite beneath the monastery. They had been dragging people into the walls. Human sacrifices, to help them survive. They couldn't see the sun any more – they had to depend on the flesh of people who had recently walked on the surface of the earth, and looked into Awen's eye.

"Some of the victims' bones were completely encased in rock or brick, but the reason why so many of them were only half-buried was because they were priests and they were wearing crucifixes ... and the Druid spirits didn't have the power to suck in the symbol of the crucified Christ.

"There was another case in Wales, something in the early 1800s. The skeletons of three young men were discovered in Caerphilly Castle, and again they were half-buried in solid stone.

"This, however – ," he said, waving at the map they had drawn – "this beats everything."

"What do you think we ought to do?" asked Lucy. "Our friend Courtney wants to call the police but we're not so sure. We don't think that they're going to believe us."

"No, well, they won't, will they? You might be lucky and find one detective who believes you. His superior officer might be persuaded, too. But if they're going to bring a prosecution against your Mr Vane, it'll have to be referred to the Crown Prosecution Service, and I can't see anybody *there* risking their career to prosecute anybody for making human sacrifices to ancient Druid spirits, can you?"

"But if it's the only possible explanation..." John began.

Uncle Robin shook his head. "I've been studying Druids and Druidic lore for thirty years, John, and I know what they were capable of doing. But I gave up trying to persuade other people a long time ago. People don't want to believe that there's such a thing as magic. They don't want to think that there are other worlds, right beneath their feet. It rattles them.

"When my book came out *The Sunday Times* said it was 'mumbo-jumbo'. Since then I haven't written another word on the subject and I've learned to keep my mouth shut. Until now, that is."

"We have to stop Mr Vane somehow."

"For your own protection, yes, you do. But right at this moment I don't exactly know how. I need to do some more research for you ... and you can do some research, too. Find out who Mr Vane actually is, where he comes from, some of his background.

"There are three things that we can do. First, we can gather enough information on Mr Vane's connection with these skeletons to have him prosecuted for being an accessory to murder. I'm not very optimistic about that, but we can try. Second, we can find a way to break the link between the houses so that the Druid spirits can't use them any longer. Again, I don't think there's much chance of that, because the ley lines are so strong. Third, we find a way to deal with Mr Vane."

"Deal with him? What do you mean?"

"Put him out of the property business, for good."

"You mean *kill* him?"

"Of course not. I'm an anthropologist, John, not a hit man. But I don't think he deserves very much sympathy if he's been doing what you think he's been doing – selling houses to young families so that they can be offered to his spirit friends like sacrificial lambs."

Lucy said, "I'll see what I can find out about Mr Vane. I've got a friend who works in the library and she's very keen on local history and family trees and stuff like that."

"I'll get in touch with some experts on ley lines," said Uncle Robin. "There was a TV programme about them not too long ago ... I'll see if I can find out who did it."

"I'll go and check some more houses," said John.

"What about the statue?"

"Don't worry, we'll be careful."

Uncle Robin said, "That's another thing. I've never heard of a living statue before, not in Druidic lore. I'm going to have to find out what it is and what we can do to stop it. It won't be much use getting rid of Mr Vane if you've got that statue hunting you down for the rest of your life."

John thought of that line in *The Rime of the Ancient Mariner* about the traveller on a lonely road who "turns no more his head ... because he knows a frightful fiend doth close behind him tread." He was still frightened by what was happening. He still dreaded seeing the statue again, and going into Mr Vane's houses. But now that he was beginning to understand what was happening, he felt that he could cope with his fear.

He finished his tea and gave Lucy a kiss. Uncle Robin clapped him on the back and said, "You keep your eyes open, young man. We don't want anything untoward to happen to you, do we?"

John caught the bus back to Streatham High Road. It took him a few minutes of pacing up and down before he plucked up the courage to walk back into the office of Blight, Simpson & Vane, but eventually he opened the door and marched right in. Mr Cleat was standing by one of the filing cabinets and gave him a reptilian look of surprise.

"That was a very rapid recovery," he remarked.

John gave a loud pretend sniff and said, "It's only a cold. I thought I'd come and share it with everybody else."

"There is no 'everybody else' today," said Mr Cleat. "Liam is still off sick, Lucy has the same cold as you, and Courtney is meeting some clients. Perhaps you'd like to make us some tea."

"All right, then."

"No sugar for Mr Vane."

John glanced towards Mr Vane's office door and a chilling sensation ran through his nerves.

"Mr Vane's here?"

"Anything wrong with that? He's had some clients around this morning. He's got more tomorrow, too."

"Clients? You mean he's been showing them one of his houses?"

"66 Mountjoy Avenue, as a matter of fact."

"But you said that 66 Mountjoy Avenue wasn't in a fit state for viewing."

"We've had the cleaners in since then," said Mr Cleat, in his most patronizing voice.

John thought: *This is it. I can't go on pretending any longer.* He reached into his pocket and took out

Mr Rogers' ring. He held it up right in front of Mr Cleat's face.

"Well?" said Mr Cleat, trying to focus on it. "What's that supposed to be?"

"It's Mr Rogers' wedding ring. Three guesses where I found it."

Mr Cleat opened and closed his mouth two or three times. "You didn't go *into* the house, did you?"

John nodded. "I found it upstairs on the landing. Lucy was with me. She's a witness."

"You didn't mention it to the police when they came round here."

"No, because I didn't think that they would take my word against yours. And because we wanted more time to find out about Mr Vane's special list."

"There's nothing to find out," said Mr Cleat, dismissively. "It's a list of properties, that's all."

"They aren't just ordinary properties, though, are they?"

"Listen, John, all you need to do is to come to work promptly, do your work properly, mind your manners and mind your own business."

"You know I can't do that, don't you, now that I know what happened to Mr Rogers."

"Well, I don't honestly think that you *do* know what happened to Mr Rogers – so if you'd like to give me that ring I can make sure that his widow gets it back and I think that we can forget the whole matter, don't you?"

"His *widow*?" asked John. "He's only missing. Nobody's said that he's dead."

"Just a slip of the tongue," said Mr Cleat. "I'll have the ring back, anyway."

"Mr Cleat," said John, and his heart was thumping so hard that he was sure that Mr Cleat could hear it. "You know what happened to Mr Rogers and I know what happened to Mr Rogers. The same thing that happened to all those people in Laverdale Square."

Mr Cleat smoothed his hair back, again and again. He glanced at Mr Vane's door. "I can't discuss it," he said. "Give me the ring."

John shook his head. "They were all sucked in by the walls, weren't they? That's what happened to them."

Mr Cleat was so agitated that John wasn't afraid of him any longer – especially when he leaned closer and spoke to John in a hoarse, quick whisper. "It wasn't my fault, John. I tried to get to Mr Rogers in time, but I got held up in traffic. Who knows? He might have been all right. Sometimes the houses don't take people for weeks or even months. But when I got there, he was gone. There was absolutely nothing that I could do."

"So you've known all along what Mr Vane's houses do to people?"

Mr Cleat puckered his mouth. "I did my best to save Mr Rogers. It was the traffic."

"You've known all along what they do to people and you don't even *care* about it? You've never tried to stop him? There were more than fifty skeletons in that house in Laverdale Square. Women and children, too."

"John, I know. But for goodness' sake – they were well before my time, most of them, from what I've read. Victorian, Edwardian, 1920s. You can't blame me for things that happened long before I was born."

John said, "I didn't think you knew, Mr Cleat. At least I *hoped* you didn't know."

"Well, I didn't know for quite some time. In fact, it took me three or four years to find out. After all, why should I suspect anything? Once you've sold a house to somebody, you very rarely see them again, do you? How do you know if they've disappeared?

"Apart from that, there was nothing to arouse my suspicions, was there? Mr Vane's properties didn't change hands unusually quickly. Some of them didn't come back on the market for five or ten years, and it never occurred to me that they were standing empty. How was I to know the owners had vanished within two or three months of moving in? Sometimes it was only a matter of days. Sometimes, probably, hours."

"But even when you found out what was going on, you still went on working for Mr Vane?"

"What else was I supposed to do? You know for yourself how difficult it is to get anybody to believe you. I called the police once, in the early days, when a family of seven went missing. They searched the property but back then I didn't have any idea *where* the people had gone, and so I didn't suggest that they knock down the walls. It wasn't until they demolished that house in Laverdale Square that I suddenly realized. It was a considerable shock, let me tell you."

"And you're not going to resign, or say anything, even now?"

Mr Cleat's nostrils quivered. "It isn't as easy as all that. Mr Vane has done me certain favours in the past. He wouldn't accept my notice even if I handed it in."

He paused, and then he said, "There's something else, too. A local news reporter tried to investigate Mr Vane's special list, five or six years ago. They found his body down by Streatham Common station, on the railway embankment. The police said that he was so badly battered that it looked as if a load of timber had fallen on top of him."

The statue, thought John. *If you start poking your nose into Mr Vane's business, that's what happens. He sends the statue to take care of you.*

157

Less than ten minutes later, Mr Vane came out of his office. He was wearing a black double-breasted suit and he looked even more skeletal than ever. He looked John up and down and said, "Well, well, well. I was told you had taken to your bed."

"I'm much better now, thanks."

Mr Vane went to the filing cabinet and pulled out one of the drawers. "I understand that you've been very busy," he said. "I wouldn't like to overwork you."

"I've just been doing some homework," John replied.

Mr Vane approached him and gave him a strange, almost affectionate smile. "You ought to have been more selective, perhaps, about whose homes you were working on."

He might have been smiling, but Mr Vane had a coldness about him which was like an open fridge. "I think it's time I gave you a little personal training, John. After all, I've been in this business for a very long time. Why don't you come along with me tomorrow when I take my clients to 66 Mountjoy Avenue?"

"Erm ... I think I'm busy tomorrow. Mr Cleat wants me to tidy up the files."

"The files can wait. You need some on-the-job experience. You need to see how a professional goes about selling a house."

"Well, Courtney's shown me quite a lot."

"Courtney's good, yes. But a little too *pushy*, in my opinion. You must stand back and allow your client to do all the work. Let him sell the house to himself. That way, he will always offer you a much higher price."

John didn't know what to say. His heart was beating so loudly that he was sure that Mr Vane could hear it. Mr Cleat said, "It's a very good offer. Mr Vane's one of the best."

Mr Vane slowly rotated his head around – almost like Megan in *The Exorcist* – and gave Mr Cleat a long, chilly look. "It's not an *offer*, David. It's an instruction." Then he rotated his head back and said to John, "I'll be meeting my clients outside the property at four-thirty precisely tomorrow afternoon. Make sure you're punctual, make sure your shoes are polished, and don't say anything unless I tell you to."

"All right, Mr Vane. Thanks, Mr Vane."

Mr Vane turned around and gave him an even wider and yellower smile than before. "Don't mention it, John. Don't mention it."

It was then that John looked over Mr Vane's shoulder and caught sight of somebody waving frantically to him from the front door. It was Courtney. He was holding up a bunch of keys, and John suddenly understood what must have happened. He had borrowed Mr Vane's keys while he was out with his clients at 66 Mountjoy Avenue, and taken them along to the hardware store to be copied. But Mr Vane had returned before the keys were finished, and any second now he was going to go back to his desk and discover that they were gone.

Mr Vane looked at his watch. His wrist was as thin and scaly as a turkey's claw. "I'd better be going now," he said. He reached into his pocket and produced the keys to 66 Mountjoy Avenue. He hesitated, and then he said, "I might as well take these with me. I won't have to come into the office tomorrow to pick up those new particulars, will I? Young John here can bring them out to me."

He smiled at John again. "Half-past four, remember? Absolutely on the dot."

14

After he had gone, Courtney came into the office and sat down at his desk and said, "*Fwooff!* That was close!"

Mr Cleat said, "What was close?"

John held out his hand for the keys. Courtney frowned and shook his head and whispered, "What are you doing?" but John said, "Come on. Cleaty's on our side now."

"What?" said Courtney, in disbelief.

John continued to hold out his hand and Courtney reluctantly gave him two big bunches of assorted keys, the originals and the copies. John held them up so that Mr Cleat could see them, and said, "Now we can get into every single house on

Mr Vane's special list. We can check them all for evidence, and if we find what we're looking for, then we can call the police."

Mr Cleat came up and John gave him all the original keys. He looked even more haggard than ever. "I hope you realize you're signing your own dismissal notice? If Mr Vane has to give up this business, then we're all out on our ears."

"You're worried about your job?" said John. "Liam lost more than his job."

"What are you talking about? Liam's off sick, that's all."

John said, "No, he isn't," and he told Mr Cleat everything that had happened at 93 Madeira Terrace. Mr Cleat slowly sat down, his eyes filling with tears.

"The other people ... the people who bought Mr Vane's houses ... the ones who disappeared ... I never knew their names ... I never knew who they were. But this ... Liam—"

"Did it make any difference, not knowing their names?" Courtney demanded.

"Well, it shouldn't have done, should it?" said Mr Cleat, wiping his eyes and noisily blowing his nose. "But I was frightened, I suppose."

"Everybody gets frightened, man," said Courtney. "It's when you stand up to your fear, that's what makes all the difference."

Mr Cleat sniffed and turned away, but John said,

"You'd better listen. Lucy and I think we know what's been happening."

"You mean there's a logical explanation for all of this?"

"Well, there's an explanation, but it isn't exactly logical. We've still got lots of work to do, lots of research to do."

"I hope you know what you're up against."

"I don't," said John. "But I think I'm just about to find out."

That evening he phoned his father from Uncle Robin's house and told him that he was spending another night away.

"Is there something wrong, son? You're not in trouble?"

"I'm fine, Dad. I'm just making new friends."

"You'll be back tomorrow, though? Your mum's missing you."

"Tell her I miss her, too."

Lucy came in from the kitchen, where she had been making shepherd's pie. "Everything all right?"

John nodded. "Fine. I feel fine. I don't know what's happened to me today. I stood up to Cleaty and he just fell apart like a box of wet Kleenex."

"Cleaty's all right. He's just like most people. More scared than they ought to be."

"And you're not? If that statue finds us..."

At that moment, they heard the key in the latch.

Uncle Robin came in with two large books and a bundle of papers under his arm. "Success, I think," he said, and gave them the thumbs-up.

After supper, they sat around the kitchen table. Uncle Robin opened his books and spread out his papers. "I went to see this chap in Croydon today – he was the one who made that documentary on Druids. I didn't tell him what was going on, but he said that there have been literally scores of unexplained disappearances in England and Wales over the past hundred years. Whole families have vanished without any trace at all – and their houses have always been on recognized ley lines.

"It's a known phenomenon – but up until now, everybody put it down to natural causes."

Lucy said, "Hasn't anybody ever put two and two together?"

"Oh, yes. There have been dozens of books and articles about ley lines, connecting them with unexplained disappearances, but none of them have ever been taken seriously. Bit like UFO abductions, really."

"But this man believes in it?"

"Believes in it? He's passionate about it. He said that when the original Druids dispersed and died out, their spirits lived on, along the ley lines; and so their influence on the British countryside remained enormous. They still control all the magical highways that connect one sacred site with another.

They still have an influence on weather, and crop-fertility, and fate.

"In the early days, people in England and Wales buried their dead along ley lines as an offering to the Druid spirits that lived on under the ground. In fact, the whole practice of burial arose because we were offering our dead to the Druid priesthood, in the hope that they wouldn't try to take the living."

"This bloke," said John, "did he give you any idea how we could *stop* these spirits? I mean, can't we exorcize them or something?"

Lucy said, "If the ley lines are like highways, isn't there a way we could make them change course, you know, like a diversion, or block them off?"

Uncle Robin shook his head, "That's like trying to stop the tides or postpone the night. The ley lines are a huge natural force, like streams of pure primeval energy. But there might be one hope.

"At Mont St Michel, the monks got rid of the Druid spirits buried in the rock beneath them, even though they did it by accident. They drove a series of iron spikes into the granite to support their new foundations, and one night there was a huge thunderstorm. Lightning struck the iron spikes – which sent a huge electrical charge deep into the mountain.

"I don't know whether the lightning destroyed the spirits or whether it simply drove them away.

But from that time on, the monastery was never troubled by any more disappearances or strange noises or anything.

"The Romans must have known about the effect of lightning on ley lines, too. Look here – this is a contemporary account by Suetonius Paulinus, who massacred the last Druids in Anglesey in AD 61. *Even after death the Druids threatened our settlements, pulling men and women into the very earth as sacrifices. We learned from living Druids, under pain of torture, that their spirits could be expunged from the underground paths through which they travelled by the power of lightning.*

"What the Romans did was to thrust their spears into the ground wherever a ley line ran, and wait for the spears to be struck by lightning."

"Well, that's something, isn't it?" said John. "I bet you that we could find a way to direct a lightning strike into one of Mr Vane's houses."

"We probably could. But it's a bit of a long shot."

"So what? It's still worth a try."

"I've also found out about the statue," said Uncle Robin. "The Druid spirits can rise up out of the earth, into the roots of an oak tree, and occupy the trunk and the branches. That allows them to see the sun, which they need to rejuvenate their strength and their magical powers. But of course an oak tree can't move.

"In AD 1457, however, after some kind of divine revelation, the Order of Druids employed sixteen craftsmen to make them a jointed statue. Apparently it was a perfect replica of Aedd Mawr, the man who founded the Druids in 1000 BC. It was made out of oak, with an ivory face. This sounds an awful lot like *your* statue, don't you agree?"

"They made only one?" asked Lucy. "We saw them all over the place."

"So far as the history books tell it, there *was* only one. But this one statue allowed the Druid spirits to rise up out of the ground and to walk wherever they wanted. You see, they could enter the oak statue in just the same way that they could enter an oak tree. But unlike the oak tree, the statue isn't rooted into the earth. It can move. It can run after you. Not only that, it can travel along ley lines like a stone from Stonehenge.

"That's how it was able to turn up outside your house, John, and then almost immediately afterwards appear at Lucy's flat. It took the fastest route through south London – the ley line. That's why it didn't even need a key to get in. It came through the ground, see. Right through the earth."

He paused. "You're privileged, in a way. You've had Aedd Mawr after you, the greatest of all the Druids. The most vengeful. The one most likely to tear you limb from limb."

"Oh, yes, some privilege," said John. "But how can we stop something like that?"

Uncle Robin said, "I asked my two experts, but neither of them knew. And I have to confess that I don't know, either. Maybe you can chop it up with a hatchet. Maybe you can stop it with a spell. But there aren't any records of anybody ever confronting it, and if they did, they didn't live to tell the tale. I'm sorry. I really am."

"That's all right," said John. "I think you've done really well."

Lucy said, "I wish *I* had. I went to Streatham library and I managed to find out a few things about Mr Vane. Not very much. Everybody seems to know him, you know, but nobody seems to know very much about him. He's always invited to give away the prizes at flower shows, that's what it says in the local papers. He's a member of the Streatham Rotarians, but he never seems to go to any of the meetings.

"I checked the electoral register. His full name is Raven Vigo Vane and he lives at 6 St Helier Street, Streatham. He's the only voter in the house, but that doesn't necessarily mean that he's the only person who lives there.

"I also talked to my friend Gloria who works for the local paper. She's going to go in early tomorrow and see if she can find out anything else," said Lucy. "They've got files that go back over a hundred years."

"That's very good," said Uncle Robin. "But I hope it doesn't take too long. Remember that John is supposed to be meeting Mr Vane at half-past four tomorrow, and I think it would help him a lot if he had a fair idea of what he's really up against."

"I don't think that you should go, John," Lucy told him. "It's obvious that Mr Vane knows what we've been up to. He's going to try to make you disappear – just like Liam disappeared, and all of those other people."

"The difference is that I'm going to be ready for him," said John.

"Yes, and he's going to be ready for you."

"I know. But it's the only way. Somehow we have to trick him into admitting what he's been doing, and if I don't go, I won't have a chance of getting him to do that. If I carry a mobile phone, and keep it connected to *your* mobile phone, then you could record everything he says without him even realizing it."

"Well, that doesn't sound like a bad idea," said Uncle Robin. "And if anything goes wrong, Lucy and I could be waiting close by. Sort of a back-up squad."

They talked until well past one in the morning. They drank hot chocolate and then Uncle Robin opened a bottle of red wine. They talked about the statue, and Druids, but even with his heavily-bruised shoulder, John still found it all too hard to believe. "It looks like a man and it moves like a man, but when you see it close up its face still looks as if it's carved out of ivory. It's totally scary."

He had seen the statue and he had seen Liam taken right in front of his eyes. Yet he still found it difficult to believe that they were fighting against three-thousand-year-old Druid spirits.

How could spirits have survived for so long underneath the earth? How could they have tolerated such an endless existence, trapped inside walls and rocks and burial stones? All John could think of was claustrophobia. Yet the Druid spirits must be everywhere – everywhere you walk. You probably couldn't walk across a field anywhere without crossing a ley line. Wherever you went, there were hungry spirits seething in the earth beneath your feet.

"The houses are the key to all this," said Uncle Robin. "The houses are the Druids' sacrificial temples. When the Romans destroyed the Druid religion, they made sure that they knocked down all the Druid temples and scattered their sacred stones."

"We can't knock down Mr Vane's houses. There are twenty-seven of them."

"I know ... but if we could just find out more about them. I mean, what makes them different from other houses ... what makes it possible for the Druid spirits to live inside their walls."

He paused, thoughtfully, and then he said, "I think I'll pay a visit to a builder pal of mine tomorrow morning. He's been putting up houses in Streatham for the past thirty years. Perhaps *he'll* have some ideas."

Lucy said, "The only thing I know about those houses is that they frighten me half to death."

15

John was dreaming that he was lost in a dark forest of oak trees when he heard a loud knocking noise. At first he thought that someone was knocking in his dream, but then he heard Uncle Robin's bedroom door open, and the landing light was switched on.

The knocking was repeated. *Bang – bang – bang!* It seemed as if the whole house shook.

"All right, all right, keep your hair on," said Uncle Robin, as he went down the stairs.

Bang – bang – bang! John sat up in bed and suddenly he had a deep feeling of dread. Who would beat so loudly on Uncle Robin's front door at two o'clock in the morning if they didn't have seriously bad news – or wanted something so urgently that they couldn't wait until the morning?

He pushed back the covers and climbed out of bed. He picked up his jeans, which he had thrown over the doll with the leprous face to stop her from staring at him in the moonlight. Still buttoning them up, he opened his bedroom door and looked out on to the landing.

Bang – bang – bang! The knocking was so loud this time that the sash window over the stairs rattled in its frame.

"For goodness' sake, I'm coming," said Uncle Robin, and slid the chain off the front door.

"Uncle Robin!" called John. "Ask who it is first!"

Uncle Robin glanced up at him. "Yes, you're probably right." He paused, with his hand on the latch. "Who is it?"

Bang – bang – bang!

"I said, who is it, and what do you want? You can't go knocking on people's doors at this time of the ni—"

With a smash, the door burst open, throwing Uncle Robin up against the wall. Framed in the darkness stood the statue, its calm eyes staring directly up the staircase at John.

Uncle Robin climbed unsteadily on to his feet, holding his head in both hands. He stared at the statue and it was plain by the look on his face that he knew what it was, but all he could do was to open his mouth and close it again, without uttering a word.

The statue stepped into the hallway. It was so tall that its monkish hood brushed against the lampshade and set the light swinging backwards and forwards, so that one moment its ivory face was brightly illuminated and the next it was plunged into shadow. It grasped the bannister with one gloved hand, and took a step upwards. It was just as supple as a living man, yet it was so heavy that it made the stairs creak.

John was paralyzed for five full seconds. He couldn't move. He couldn't breathe. All he could do was watch the statue slowly climbing the stairs towards him, and the light swinging backwards and forwards.

His fear rose and rose like the red line in a thermometer. Then suddenly it reached a point where it burst and launched him into action. He threw himself across the landing, hurled open Lucy's bedroom door, and screamed at her, "*Lucy! The statue! It's found us!*"

He slammed the bedroom door shut behind him and twisted the key in the lock. He heard the statue reach the landing and turn towards him. Lucy was sitting up in bed blinking at him in shock. "*Come on!*" he told her. "*We've got to get out of here! Quick!*"

Lucy staggered out of bed. She was wearing only

a long striped nightshirt. "My clothes—" she said, but at that moment there was a thunderous knock at the door. Plaster showered down on either side of the frame, and the panels started to splinter.

"Forget about your clothes! It's going to kill us!"

John went to the window, unlocked it, and lifted it upward. Just below the sill there was the narrow sloping roof of Uncle Robin's front porch. John clambered out. The porch roof was so steeply angled that his feet slid down to the guttering, and he was only able to save himself from falling by clutching on to the drainpipe.

"Come on!" he urged Lucy. She hesitated, but then there was another devastating crash at the door, and she climbed out after him.

"I'm slipping!" she panicked.

"Just take hold of my hand – that's it. Now slide right down as far as you can."

John heaved himself over the edge of the roof, clung on to the guttering for two or three seconds, and then dropped into the front garden. He landed right on top of a gaggle of gnomes, scattering them in all directions. Lucy followed him – dangling from the gutter until he caught hold of her legs and helped her to drop to the ground.

Uncle Robin was still standing in the hallway, looking dazed.

"Go!" he told them. He took down Lucy's keys from the hook by the mirror. "Go on, go!"

"What about you?"

There was a wrenching noise from the open window of Lucy's bedroom, and then the sound of heavy oak feet crossing the floor. The statue appeared, staring down at them with terrifying equanimity.

"I'll be all right," said Uncle Robin. "It's you that it's looking for, not me."

And sure enough, the statue disappeared from the window and they heard it coming back out on to the landing.

"*Go!*" urged Uncle Robin. "Call me in the morning as soon as you can. We're going to beat this Mr Vane of yours if it's the last thing we ever do!"

Lucy's ankle was still painful, but she was able to drive. They swerved away from Uncle Robin's house and headed south, across Mitcham Common. Their single headlight made the trees and the bushes look as if they were cut out of cardboard.

John turned around. "Uncle Robin was right. It hasn't hurt him at all. It's coming out of the garden gate now. It probably wants to see which way we're going."

"Where do we go now?" asked Lucy. "I can't wake up any of my friends, not at this time of the morning."

"It's all right. It's a warm night. We can park on the common and sleep in the car."

She glanced at him. "You'd better not snore."

He didn't snore. In fact he didn't even sleep. He sat in the front passenger seat while she slept in the back, his eyes sore with tiredness, but he simply couldn't drop off. Every time he saw a bush swaying, every time he saw a tree dipping its branches, he imagined that it was the statue, still coming after them, determined to beat them to death.

The moon sank. The sky lightened. A man cycled past and stared at them so intently that he almost fell off his bike.

John and Lucy ventured back to Uncle Robin's house at about half-past six but there was no sign of the statue anywhere, except for the damage it had caused. Uncle Robin had managed to screw the front door back into place. He was obviously shocked, but he was full of determination.

He sat in the kitchen with a cup of tea. "Hitler couldn't frighten me out of my house and no Druid statue is going to frighten me out of my house, either."

Lucy stayed for a while to have a bath while John went off to Streatham. By nine o'clock the morning was bright and dusty and very hot. When John arrived at the office Mr Cleat was sitting at his desk with a stack of particulars in front of him and a ballpen in his hand but he was neither reading nor writing. He was staring across the office at a wasp that was crawling up the wall.

"Morning, Mr Cleat. Another hot one."

Mr Cleat nodded.

"Would you like a cup of coffee, Mr Cleat?"

"What? Oh, no. No, thank you."

"Is everything all right, Mr Cleat?"

Mr Cleat put down his pen. "Not really," he said. "And I think you can understand why."

"It wasn't your fault, Mr Cleat."

"Wasn't it? All those people ... there must have been hundreds of them. And poor Liam, too. I don't know what I'm going to say to his parents. I didn't sleep a wink last night."

You weren't the only one, thought John. But then he said, "It's no use worrying about it. Worrying isn't going to bring them all back. We have to stop Mr Vane from doing it again."

"I don't know how you're going to manage that."

"We just have to prove that he *knew* what his houses did to people, and that's why he sold them. *Then* we can go to the police. You'll give evidence against him, won't you?"

Mr Cleat gave John a twitchy little glance. "I don't know ... I did something once that Mr Vane knows about. If I spoke up against him ... well, I'd be in a lot of hot water, too."

"You *did* something? What?"

"Well, I don't want to go into too much detail, but one of our clients was a very old lady. A week before she died she altered her will and left me quite a lot of money."

"What's wrong with that?"

"The circumstances were a little irregular, that's all."

"What? You mean, you *forged* it?"

Mr Cleat sucked in his cheeks. "That's rather a direct way of putting it. But, yes, I wrote her name for her on her behalf. She was only going to donate the money to the Donkey Sanctuary, and I suppose I thought that I was a worthier charity than a field full of broken-down donkeys."

He paused. "The only trouble was, the day before she died, the old lady had a sudden moment of lucidity. She called the office to remind me that all of her money *had* to go to the donkeys. She thought she was talking to me, but I was out that day, and she spoke to Mr Vane. He didn't tell anybody what I had done, but he never misses an opportunity to remind me."

"That's blackmail, isn't it?"

"Perhaps it is. But it would be very hard to prove. Mr Vane hasn't tried to extort any money out of me and he hasn't directly threatened me. But he does expect my absolute loyalty and my absolute discretion."

He paused for a moment, and then he said,

"However, if there is anything I can do to assist you and Lucy to close down the special list for good and all ... then you can count on me."

"Thanks, Mr Cleat."

"Let's not stand on formality, John. I've made a clean breast of things now. Call me David."

Lucy came in just after half-past eleven. Mr Cleat and Courtney had both gone out on appointments so they were alone in the office together.

"I think we've come up with something," said Lucy, holding up a large brown envelope. "Uncle Robin called up his builder friend, and his builder friend had this book on south London in Victorian times."

She took it out of the envelope and opened it up at a torn paper marker. "We looked up Laverdale Square and Abingdon Gardens and Mountjoy Avenue. Well ... they don't show any photographs of Laverdale Square – but look at this."

She pointed to a sepia photograph of several top-hatted men in black frock coats standing outside a large newly-built house. The road was unpaved, and a horse and carriage stood on one side.

"You don't know where it is? Read the caption."

Mountjoy Avenue, SW – the directors of Messrs Voice Bros outside one of their quality suburban mansions in July, 1897.

"That's number 66," said John. "I didn't recognize it without all of those bushes."

"Unfortunately the men were moving so you can't clearly see their faces. But when you look up Voice Bros in the index, you get this." She opened the book at another paper marker, and read:

" 'In the 1890s, Messrs Voice Bros gained a considerable reputation for building large suburban houses of exceptional quality and value. They were extremely selective about the sites that they chose, and the construction materials which they employed, frequently bringing in stone from Wiltshire and Somerset to enhance their window frames and their interiors.

" 'They won several awards for their houses, including the Dobson Cup from the Institute of Chartered Architects, seen here being presented to Mr Charles Voice at the Royal Albert Hall.' "

Below the text there was another photograph of men in top hats and frock coats, but this time their faces were clearly visible. A portly man with large side-whiskers was presenting the cup. Accepting it, with an expression completely devoid of any humour, was a tall, thin man with slicked back hair.

"*It can't be*," said John, peering at it more closely. "This was taken over a hundred years ago."

"It could be his grandfather, I suppose. But if his grandfather was called Voice, then *he* would be called Voice, too, instead of Vane."

John said, "Do you mind if I make a copy of this?"

"Of course not."

He set the Xerox to "magnify × 10". In a few seconds, out came a huge enlargement of Mr Charles Voice receiving the Dobson Cup, and there was no doubt about it at all. It was Mr Raven Vane. Not a relative. Not a double. He even had the same mole on the left side of his chin.

"It's him," said John. "And he looks exactly the same as he does today."

"Uncle Robin's friend said he remembers Voice Bros. They went on building quality houses until the 1960s, but they refused to use modern building techniques like prefabricated panels and chipboard flooring and in the end they priced themselves out of the market."

Courtney came back into the office, carrying his lunch – two vegetable samosas and a large bottle of Coca-Cola. "Everything all right?" he asked them. "You look as if you've see a ghost."

"Perhaps we have," said John, and held up the Xerox. "Who do you think this is?"

"Mr Vane, of course. Why?"

"This picture was taken in 1898."

"What?"

"Take a look at it. September, 1898."

Courtney frowned at it and approached it closely. Lucy showed him the book. He studied it for a very long time and then said, "There can't be any question, can there? It *is* him. It's incredible."

John said, "Let's think about it. If it really *is* him, then he's lived for at least a century without getting any older. It's like those Druid spirits. They've lived for nearly three thousand years without getting any older.

"And if Mr Vane has been helping them – by building them sacrificial temples, by feeding them with human sacrifices—"

"Then this could be his reward," said Courtney. "The Druids have promised him life everlasting, just like theirs."

They all stared at each other, awed by the immensity of what they might have discovered, and yet equally aware that it might be nothing more than a ridiculous mistake. After all, it was much more likely that Mr Vane had simply been Mr Voice's double.

Yet when they looked at the picture again, they were convinced. He had the same expression, the very same look in his eyes. Two men might look facially identical, but no two men ever looked out at the world in quite the same way, and certainly nobody looked out at the world in quite the same way that Mr Vane did.

"What are you going to do now?" asked Courtney.

"Keep on digging. I was looking in the library for

background information on Mr Vane. Now I'm going to start looking under Voice, too. After John's appointment, that is."

"We've got the keys," said Courtney. "Maybe I should start looking at some more of Mr Vane's houses."

"Not yet," John told him. "It's too dangerous, just at the moment."

"Well, I'd like to do *something*. I can't let Liam get killed and do nothing about it at all."

"You can do something. You can lend me your mobile phone this afternoon. We're going to see if I can get Mr Vane to admit what he's been doing, and record it."

Courtney unclipped his phone from his belt. "Here – good luck. And don't trust that man a single inch. I can't come along with you, because I've got two viewing appointments. But if you really need me, just call me on my pager. I promise you, man, I'll drop everything and I'll be there."

16

Lucy drove him to the end of Mountjoy Avenue, with Uncle Robin sitting in the back.

"Listen!" said Uncle Robin. The afternoon was swelteringly hot and the sky was the colour of tarnished bronze. But in the distance, they could hear the deep grumble of thunder. "Sounds like we're in for a storm."

John climbed out of the car. "Be careful," Lucy warned him. He gave her a thumbs-up, even though he was feeling far from confident.

Uncle Robin said, "Just remember – one shout for help and we'll come running."

John dialled Lucy's number on Courtney's mobile phone. Lucy's phone warbled and she answered it.

"It's me. Can you hear me all right?"

"Fine. Loud and clear."

"OK, then. Get the tape recorder ready."

John walked down the road towards number 66. By the time he got there, his shirt was sticking to his back and his underpants felt like wet swimming trunks.

Mr Vane had already arrived. His black Rover was parked in the driveway, with its black tinted windows closed tight. As John approached, one of the windows slid down and Mr Vane's skull-like face appeared. "You're late," he said. He must have had the air-conditioning in his car turned to "Arctic", because a wave of cold came out of the window that made John shiver.

"Sorry. It was the bus."

"You should make provision for the vagaries of public transport."

"Yeah, I suppose I should. Yesss." He couldn't take his eyes off Mr Vane. He was even more like "Charles Voice" in the flesh than John could have imagined. There was no question in his mind now that he was one and the same man.

Mr Vane looked at his watch. "We've got five or ten minutes to spare. Would you care to see inside?"

"All right. If you want."

"It's what *you* want that's important," said Mr Vane. He closed his window and then slid out of his car like a shadow sliding under a doorway. He laid his hand on John's shoulder and guided him towards the front door. The two stone lions stood patiently on either side of the steps while time and the weather gradually blurred their features and covered them in moss. *Unlike some people I know*, thought John.

"This particular property was built in 1908, so how would you describe it?"

John looked up at it. "Bit of an old dump, I suppose."

"Not exactly, John. Not when you're trying to sell it. It was built in 1908 during the short reign of Edward VII and so you would call it Edwardian."

He put his key in the lock. "In the estate agency business, any property that is run down is generally described as 'ripe for imaginative renovation', and any property that is ugly or impractical has what we call 'character'.

"This was once a very fine house. It was built of the finest materials to a standard that today's so-called craftsmen could never hope to match. Look at this door. It needs repainting, but it's made of solid mahogany from the Honduras, and the joinery ... it's superb."

"Voice Bros," said John.

They were in the hallway now, with its black and white chequered floor. "What do you know about Voice Bros?"

"They were a firm of local builders ... they built lots of prizewinning houses."

"Well, well. You *have* been doing your homework." There was another rumble of thunder, closer this time. The light inside the house began to dim as clouds rolled over the sun. A wind suddenly got up, and blew last autumn's dried leaves across the black and white floor.

Mr Vane walked across to the sitting-room and opened the door. He went to the large bare window and stared out at the garden.

"You could have a great future in front of you, you know."

John came up and stood beside him but said nothing.

"You could lead such a life ... you could see such things."

John said, "I don't want to be an estate agent all my life. I want to be a rock musician."

"Ah. A rock musician." Mr Vane pronounced "rock musician" as if it were a phrase in a foreign language. "You want to be famous, do you? You want your name to live for ever?"

John shrugged. "I want to make some money, mainly. You know."

"So you're not interested in immortality?" Mr Vane stood very close to John and looked directly into his eyes. Through the window, behind him, John could see the trees starting to sway.

"I know about the Druids," he said.

"The *Druids*?" said Mr Vane. He stepped away

from John and paced slowly around the room, circling the shabby chaise-longue and the overturned chair. John watched him and his mouth was so dry that he had to lick his lips. "And what do you think you know about the Druids?"

"Everything. I know all about the ley lines. I know all about the people who got sucked into the walls. I know all about the statue, too."

"That's good, John. That's very good. At least I won't have the uphill struggle of trying to persuade you that it's true."

"Then it *is* true?"

The lines on Mr Vane's brow formed a narrow V-shape, like the wake of a speedboat. "Of course it's true. What do you think you're doing here today?"

"You sent that statue after us. It nearly killed us."

"You're right, John. It nearly did. But you and Lucy escaped it, didn't you, and that's why I'm making you an offer today instead of sending my condolences to your parents."

Suddenly an immense burst of thunder detonated right over the house, and it felt as if the ceiling were falling in. John said, "I can't believe that you can *admit* it, just like that! You *admit* that you sent that statue to try and kill us! You *admit* that you've been selling these houses to people when you *knew* they were all going to die!"

"Why shouldn't I? Nobody will ever believe it. Nobody ever has. Don't think that you're the first person who has tried to bring down my little empire."

John said, "I'm leaving. I'm leaving, and believe me, I'm going to tell the police all about you and this time I'll make sure that they knock down every single one of your houses and find out just how many people you've killed!"

"And I, of course, shall deny all knowledge."

"I'm still going to try. You just watch me."

John stalked back into the hallway and opened the front door. Outside, the sky was dark and coppery green, and the first fat drops of summer rain were falling into the garden. There was a feeling of electricity in the air, and danger.

And there – as he had expected – was the statue, standing ivory-faced, its arms by its sides, waiting for him. His pulse began to quicken with fear but he knew what he had to do.

He slammed the front door and walked back into the living-room. Mr Vane was watching him with a small, amused smile.

"You can't kill me, you know," John said defiantly. "People know where I am."

"Kill you, John? I don't want to *kill* you! You have spirit, John. You have initiative. I've been looking for somebody like you for a very long time."

"I don't know what you mean."

"Then I'll tell you. In 1885, when I was twenty-seven years old, I had my own small building company in Peckham. We were building quite modest houses, really – homes for doctors and solicitors and accountants – but I like to think that we built them very well.

"I had a wife, a very dear wife, and two beautiful boys. One winter I began to feel unwell, and when I went to the doctor he told me that I had a malignancy, and that I had no more than a few months to live. I was in despair. I didn't tell my wife what was wrong with me, but I went to all kinds of faith-healers and spiritualists and herbalists."

John stayed where he was. The room was so gloomy now that all he could see of Mr Vane was a silhouette against the window. His voice crackled with age and grief.

"One day, in Salisbury, I went to a Druid doctor. He told me that I didn't have to die. All I had to do was assist the Order of Druids to rebuild their temples, and in return they would use their healing powers to save my life. He demonstrated the power of his healing by placing his hand on my cheek and removing a birthmark that had troubled me all my life.

"I adored my family. I was desperate not to die. So – foolishly, perhaps – I agreed. Nobody else had been able to help me.

"I borrowed money and formed the company of Voice Bros – although my name wasn't Voice and there were no brothers. The name came from the

Bible – when Cain has murdered Abel, and buried him in the earth, and God says '*the voice of thy brother's blood crieth unto me from under the ground.*'

"I thought it was witty, when I first dreamed it up. It was only later that I realized how ironic it was."

Lightning flickered outside, and for a split-second the living-room was lividly lit up. Mr Vane's shadow jumped up the wall behind him like some terrible Jack in the Box.

"I built my houses exactly where I was told by the Order of Druids to build them – *exactly*. In the case of this house, it's standing right on a north-south ley line. The ley line runs through the exact centre of the garden at the back and out through the front door.

"Not only did I have to be precise about position, I had to set into the fireplace of every house one of the original stones from the last Druid temple on the Isle of Thanet. Do you see here?"

He approached the huge stone fireplace. Right in the centre of its main arch was a roughly-hewn piece of natural rock, engraved with twig-shaped runes.

"These stones are what transforms these houses. They make them into a gateway, do you understand? A gateway into the past, and a gateway into another existence."

He touched the stone with his fingertips, very

reverentially. Then he turned back to John, smiling, and said, "I set up a small estate agency with two of my friends, Henry Blight and Frederick Simpson, and we put the houses on the market. We were to sell them to families with plenty of children, that's what we were told. In those days, of course, it wasn't uncommon for a family to have nine or ten children, or even more.

"My health improved day by day. By the time we sold the first house, I was in terrific shape, and my doctor pronounced that my malignancy had vanished. I felt younger and fitter than ever. And then, of course, I discovered that the house was empty, and that the family to whom I had sold it had disappeared.

"I went back to the Order of Druids and they explained to me then that my houses were not really houses at all, but sacrificial temples – places where the Old Ones could satisfy their need for youth and energy and human flesh."

"Why didn't you stop then?" asked John, trying to hold up Courtney's mobile phone without making it look too obvious. "Why didn't you tell them to shove their sacrificial temples? Why didn't you pull down your houses and refuse to have anything more to do with them?"

Thunder cracked the sky from side to side. Mr Vane stood with his head lowered. "Because I didn't, John. Because I knew that if I did, my illness would return, and I would die. I was still so young. I loved my wife and my family more than I can tell you."

"You certainly loved them more than hundreds of other people."

"They were just *people*, John! When you've lived as long as I have, you begin to understand! People come and people go! Millions of people die from disease! Millions of people are cut down in wars! They're like wheat, being harvested! The sickle sweeps and down they go!"

"So what are you?" John demanded. "You're just a person, aren't you? Isn't it time that somebody harvested you?"

"Believe it or not, that's what I'm proposing. I've had enough of this life, John. I made a bargain with the Druids and I'm weary of keeping it. When they said that I wouldn't die, I didn't realize that I would *never* die. I've seen my beloved wife grow old, and buried her. I've buried my sons. I've buried my grandchildren. I've seen my friends grow from vigorous young men into creeping geriatrics. I used to think that living for ever would be wonderful. But I'm sick of it, John. I'm sick of the loneliness, and I'm sick of this business. I've been sick of it for a very long time. But up until now – up until *you* came along – I've never found any young man who was prepared to believe that what I was doing was true."

He took a deep, harsh breath. "Take my place, John. Take over the business. You, too, can live for as long as you like. One hundred years, two hundred years. You could still be alive in the year 2100!"

"Oh, yes?" John demanded. "And how many people would I have killed by then? How many people have *you* killed? Hundreds? Thousands?"

"The choice is yours, John. I didn't invite you to get involved in any of this. You poked your nose into something that was nothing to do with you, and it had tragic consequences. Poor Liam. That was all your fault."

Underneath the rumbling of the thunderstorm and the pattering of the rain, John thought that he could hear something else – a *whispering*, a *rustling*, as if dozens of people were moving swiftly all around the house, as if people were running barefoot from room to room. He could almost feel the draught as they passed him by. He could almost *see* them.

"You don't want to die today, do you, John? Of course you don't. But in that corny old cliché of crime fiction, John, you know far too much. Quite a few of my employees have known too much, in the past, but not many of them have had the persistence or the intelligence to do anything about it. You frighten me, John, because if I let you walk out of this house today, you might find a way to prove what I've done, and I can't let you do that."

John said, "You can do whatever you like, Mr Vane. I'm going, and that's it."

He walked back out to the hallway. He was so frightened that he felt as if his hair was bristling. He knew the statue was going to be waiting for him outside. But this time he was prepared for it – or at least, he thought he was prepared for it.

He had almost reached the door when it burst wide open right in front of him with the lock tumbling across the floor. The statue stepped in, its face calm but utterly uncompromising. It started to move towards him and it was then that John released his secret weapon. He scooped his hand into his pocket and scattered glass marbles all across the floor. They bounced and rolled everywhere, and the statue walked right into the thick of them.

But instead of losing its balance, the statue simply *crushed* the marbles underfoot, grinding them into powdery glass sugar. It kept on coming, swiftly and silently, and it pushed John in the chest with such force that he staggered back three or four paces, totally winded. It marched forward and pushed him again, so that he collided with the wall.

Gasping, he tried to dodge out of the way. But to his surprise he found that he was stuck against the wall. His back felt as if it were being tugged by dozens of grasping hands. The harder he struggled, the more powerful the tugging seemed to be.

"*No!*" he shouted. He suddenly thought of Liam being dragged into the wallpaper in Brighton with his mouth stretched open and his one eye begging.

He reached behind him and tried to push himself free from the wall, but his hand stuck to it too. He turned around and watched in horror as his fingers gradually disappeared into the yellow-painted plaster. Each finger felt stiff and numb, as if he were suffering from frostbite. Within a few seconds his whole hand had been sucked into the wall, right up to the wrist.

The statue stayed where it was, its face impassive.

"*Help me!*" John screamed. "*Don't just stand there – help me!*"

Mr Vane appeared from the living-room and approached him with a quiet, measured tread. "I made you an offer, John. You decided to turn it down. You must understand that I can't possibly let you go."

John leaned back in his efforts to pull himself from the wall, but the instant that the back of his head touched the plaster, his hair was caught, and then his scalp was pulled in.

"*No! You can't let this happen! Tell them to stop it! No!*"

Mr Vane lifted his wrist and looked at his watch.

"Don't you worry, John. It doesn't take long."

17

John screamed again and he was still screaming when the front door opened. The hallway was lit by a dazzling crackle of lightning. In the doorway stood Courtney and Mr Cleat.

"*Help me! Get me out of here! Help me!*"

Courtney made a move towards him, but Mr Vane raised his arm and shouted, "Stay back! It's too late for him now!"

But Courtney said, "It's too late for you, man! We know all about your houses and we know all about you!"

"I said *stay back!*"

Courtney took another step forward. As he did so, however, the statue turned around to face him, as fast and fluid as a boxer. Courtney tried to dodge past him but the statue swung its arm and hit him on the shoulder. Courtney was jolted back, and as he lifted his arms to defend himself, the statue hit him again and again. It caught him on the side of the head and he was knocked backward on to the floor.

Although his eyes were bulging with fright, Mr Cleat tried to circle round the statue on the right-hand side of the hall. The statue turned its head and started to move towards him, slowly lifting its right arm in the air.

Mr Cleat managed to duck to one side, and the statue's blow hit the bannisters with a sound like a cricket bat, breaking three of the uprights. It twisted around and hit out wildly, again and again, and one of its blows caught Mr Cleat right between the shoulder blades. He dropped on the floor on his hands and knees, and the statue strode up to him with both fists raised, ready to pummel him into the tiles.

At that moment, though, Courtney tried to run around the other side of the hallway. "No, you don't!" said Mr Vane, and snatched at his arm.

The statue turned its head to see what was happening. Courtney twisted himself free from Mr Vane, threw himself across the hall and collided with the statue with all his weight. The statue toppled over Mr Cleat and fell to the floor with a devastating crack. Its ivory face broke away from its head and skated across the tiles.

Blind now, the statue rose to its feet. It took two staggering steps to the right, and then three more steps to the left, swinging its arms dementedly from side to side.

"What have you done?" shouted Mr Vane. "It's Aedd Mawr, the greatest Druid of them all! What have you done!"

He went across to the statue, his hands held out to guide it. The statue collided with the wall and then blundered into the hallstand, smashing the mirror and breaking the shelves.

Mr Vane tried to take hold of its arm, but the statue swivelled around and hit him across the side of the head – a blow which almost lifted him off the ground and sent him hurtling across the hall and into the bannisters. He collapsed on to the floor with blood running down the side of his face, his arms and legs as crooked as a broken puppet.

"*Help me!*" John screamed. His arm had disappeared into the wall up to the elbow, and he could feel the terrible clawing, tugging sensation growing stronger and stronger.

Courtney took hold of his one free hand and pulled it as hard as he could. Mr Cleat seized hold of his legs.

"*Get me out!*" John panicked. "*I don't want to go into the wall like Liam! Get me out!*"

"Liam only had one person to help him," said

Courtney, gritting his teeth. "Come on, Cleaty, *pull!*"

He locked hands with John, and then he heaved back until John could hear the muscles in his arm cracking. Courtney's feet slid and scrabbled on the tiles, but at last he managed to get a purchase.

"Now *pull!*" he panted. "And *pull!*"

Mr Cleat was much stronger than John would have guessed. He tugged so hard on John's coat that he nearly tore the lapels off, but the dragging force inside the wall was almost irresistible. John's arm disappeared and he couldn't feel his hand at all. The back of his head was buried in the wall up to his ears, and he felt as if his whole brain was beginning to freeze. He felt like giving up, and allowing the wall to pull him in to get it over with.

On the other side of the hallway, the faceless statue was still stumbling around, breaking windows, splintering door panels and tearing down curtains.

Courtney said, "Come on, one last pull! Come on, Cleaty, this is for all the people who've been lost in the walls! This is for Liam!"

He counted, "One – two – three—" and then they all pulled together. Mr Cleat pulled so hard that he let out a long, high-pitched squeal of effort.

There was a moment when John was sure that they had lost him for good, and he thought of his mother and his father and Ruth. He could feel himself being relentlessly dragged into a dark, freezing-cold world where life meant nothing – a world of black superstitions and terrible rituals, a world of whispers and ghosts and dark, unspeakable memories.

He could feel himself right on the point of death.

"*Noooo!*" he screamed, although he couldn't hear himself screaming. And it was then that he made the supreme effort himself, flexing back his shoulders and forcing his head forward and wrenching his arm.

At that moment, Uncle Robin and Lucy appeared in the doorway. Lucy clamped her hand over her mouth in horror, but Uncle Robin came hurrying across the hall. As he did so, he dragged out of the pocket of his old green velvet jacket a long chain of crucifixes – some large, some small, some silver, some brass, some wooden, some plastic.

The statue heard him and swung around, but it walked straight into the stairs and fell to its knees, where it remained, motionless, as if it were praying.

Uncle Robin came over to John and looped the chain of crucifixes between him and the wall. At once, John felt the wall actually *recoil*, with a cold, plastery shudder.

"Now, let's all pull!" said Uncle Robin. "Let's all pull, and we'll get him out!"

Courtney pulled. Mr Cleat pulled. Uncle Robin

pulled. They gritted their teeth with effort. Then, with a sharp *chish!* sound like a yard-broom sweeping up concrete, John tumbled out of the wall and all four of them fell on to the floor in a tangle.

Courtney helped John on to his feet.

"Are you all right? I thought we'd lost you there, man, I really did."

Lucy turned him around. He was shivering with cold and shock, and his back was thickly covered in plaster dust. His hands were mottled blue, as if he'd been frostbitten.

"I'm all right," he told her. "Really. I'm all right."

Courtney said, "Cleaty said that we shouldn't risk it – letting you meet Mr Vane alone – so we came straight over."

"Are you *sure* you're all right?" Lucy asked John.

"Thanks to Uncle Robin," said John.

Uncle Robin gathered up his chain of crosses. "The one thing that the Druids can never swallow is the symbol of Christian faith," he said, grimly.

Mr Cleat went over to Mr Vane and lifted his chin. "Out cold," he said. "Do you think we'd better call an ambulance?"

There was another flash of lightning, followed by a burst of thunder that shook the windows in their sashes. Uncle Robin looked up and said, "There's one thing we ought to try first. We may not get the chance to do it again."

"The lightning!" said John.

"What are you talking about?" asked Courtney. "We ought to get you and Mr Vane out of here, and get you seen to."

"But the lightning!" said John, scrambling on to his feet.

"That's right," said Uncle Robin. "It's the only way to destroy a Druid spirit!"

Lucy said, "You can't! It's much too dangerous!"

"But if we don't do it now—"

"Do what? Do what?" Courtney demanded.

Uncle Robin explained how the Romans had dug their metal spears into Druid ley lines and waited for them to be struck by lightning. "The lightning went into the ley lines – and zap!"

"*Zap?*" said Mr Cleat, dubiously.

"It's worth a try! I mean, look at this thunderstorm! It may not thunder like this again for months!"

"But we don't have any spears!" Mr Cleat pointed out.

"We don't need spears," said John. "There's some scaffolding round at the side of the house. We can stick a bit in the middle of the garden, right where the ley line runs."

They went outside, into the front garden. The wind was wild and the trees were roaring. Rain lashed against their faces and soaked them through to the skin before they had even reached the side of the house.

It was completely dark, and they had to wait until there was another flash of lightning before they could see where half a dozen scaffolding poles were lying in the weeds. Courtney picked up the end of one, John took the other end, and Mr Cleat took the middle. The pole was at least six metres long and much heavier than John had expected. They carried it around to the back garden, rain running down their faces.

Lightning crackled down from the clouds. Thunder rumbled so close overhead that Lucy covered her ears and ducked her head down. Mr Cleat shouted, "Where's the ley line? I can't carry this thing very much further!"

"Exact centre of the garden, that's what Mr Vane said!" shouted John.

They carried the scaffolding pole a few metres further on, with Uncle Robin hurrying ahead of them. Suddenly he called out, "Here! Here! This is where it is! I can feel it!"

They laid the pole on the grass and gathered around him.

"Feel it!" he said. "Put your foot on the ground there and feel it!"

John took a step forward. As he did so, he immediately felt the same cold, pulling sensation that he had felt in the wall. It was like a cold hand grasping his foot and trying to drag him into the earth.

Lucy let out a frightened yelp. "Something *touched* me! Something touched my shoe!"

"I think we'd better forget this scaffolding business and get out of here," said Courtney.

"We can't!" said John. "Nobody is ever going to believe any of this, nobody except us! If we don't do something now, nobody ever will. And look, the storm is beginning to pass over!"

Mr Cleat suddenly stepped back and stamped at the ground as if he were trying to stamp on a beetle. "I can feel them, too. They're everywhere!"

"Then let's get this pole into the ground as quick as we can!"

They hefted up the pole and carried it over to the nearest flowerbed, where the earth was sodden and soft. With every step they could feel a snatching, grabbing sensation at their feet. They lifted the pole upright and together they forced it downward into the soil, pushing it and twisting it until it stayed up on its own.

As they did so, they kept shaking and kicking at the ground, to loosen the grip of the forces that wanted to drag them into the darkness.

Another flicker of lightning illuminated the garden. "Let's hope this pole doesn't get struck till we're finished," gasped Courtney.

"I don't think there's any chance that it's going to get struck at all," said Mr Cleat, wiping the rain from his face with his sleeve. "I think the best thing we can do is get out of here, fast."

They stood back. The pole wasn't entirely straight, but it looked as if it would stay where it was. They turned and started to hurry back towards the house. But they hadn't gone more than seven or eight metres before Mr Cleat shouted out, "*Ahh!*" and disappeared up to his knees into the grass.

18

John started to go to help him, but Uncle Robin said "Be careful!" and Courtney grabbed his arm and held him back.

"That's going to be just as dangerous as that wall, man. The next thing we know, we're all going to get dragged down!"

John felt a chilly tugging sensation beneath his feet, and invisible fingers coiling themselves around his ankle. He kicked them away and took a sharp step sideways.

"Get me out of here!" called Mr Cleat. "It's pulling me down, just like a swamp! I can't move my legs at all!"

Uncle Robin said, "Here! I'll throw you these crosses! Wrap them around your waist and they won't be able to drag you in any further!"

He swung the chain of crucifixes around and around and then he threw them. They fell only a few millimetres away from Mr Cleat's outstretched fingers, but as they touched the grass they were flung wildly up and away from him as if they had been repelled by a powerful magnet.

Mr Cleat made a desperate attempt to snatch them, but they were just out of his reach.

"I'll get them!" said Lucy, but Uncle Robin held her arm.

"If you go anywhere across there, the same thing will happen to you."

"I'll get another pole!" said Courtney. "Just hold on, Cleaty, we'll soon get you out of there!"

"It's pulling me down, Courtney, I'm telling you. I can't even feel my feet at all!"

John and Courtney ran back to the side of the house, picked up another scaffolding pole and carried it back to the lawn.

Lucy cried out, "Hurry! He's sinking even faster!"

Another flash of lightning lit up the bizarre sight of Mr Cleat in his business suit, standing up to his thighs in a weedy, wet, unkempt lawn. He looked as if he were wading in the sea – except that the waves were windblown billows of thistles and grass.

Mr Cleat was trying to stay calm but his self-control was gradually cracking. "John ... Courtney ... you have to get me out of here ... they keep on pulling me further down ... they keep on ... *get me out of here, for God's sake! It hurts! You can't even imagine how much it hurts!"*

John and Courtney laid the scaffolding pole across the lawn. John skirted around to the opposite side and took hold of the other end of the pole. Then they lifted it up so that Mr Cleat could reach it with both hands.

"Right, Cleaty, grab hold of the pole, and grab it tight!" shouted Courtney.

Mr Cleat did as he was told. "You'll have to be quick," he said – and he was right, because he was visibly sinking into the ground in front of their eyes. The grass had reached his waist now, and his belt-buckle had disappeared into the weeds.

Courtney ducked under the scaffolding pole so that it was supported by his shoulders, and John did the same. "Now, heave!" said Courtney, and between them they tried to raise the pole like a pair of weight-lifters.

John squeezed his eyes shut and clenched his teeth. His shoulder muscles strained so much that he could hardly bear the pain. The pole itself was heavy enough, without having Mr Cleat hanging on to it – especially since Mr Cleat was being dragged down by one of the most powerful supernatural forces ever known.

He did his best, but the weight pressing down on the back of his neck was so great that he thought the pole was going to break it. And all the time the wind was howling and the rain was blasting straight into his face and Mr Cleat was screaming, *"Get me out of here! It's killing me! Get me out of here!"*

John and Courtney both pushed up on the pole with all the strength they could muster, but gradually they were driven down on to their knees, and even lower, until their faces were being forced down into the wet grass and weeds.

"It's no use!" shouted Courtney. "We'll have to think of something else!"

He eased his head out from underneath the pole, which was now less than half a metre above the lawn. John did the same.

"What are you doing? What are you doing? You can't just let me go under!"

John said, "There was some wooden boarding next to the scaffold – maybe we could lay it flat on the lawn and crawl across it to reach him."

Mr Cleat was still desperately clinging on to the pole. *"Get me out of here! I don't want to die! John, help me, I can't even feel my legs! I can't feel anything!"*

He had sunk into the lawn right up to his chest, and he seemed to be going down faster and faster. Now that he was so deeply buried in the soil, the Druids must have had a better grip on him. At the rate they were pulling him into the ground, he had less than a minute left to escape.

"Please – don't leave me!" he sobbed. *"I know that I was wrong! I know that I'm to blame! I should have stopped him! I know I should have stopped him! But please!"*

Courtney came sprinting back from the side of the house with a large, flat scaffolder's plank. He dropped it across the lawn until it was well within Mr Cleat's reach. Mr Cleat let go of the pole and lunged out for the plank. He gripped the end of it with both hands, although the grass was up to his armpits. Between the rumbles of thunder and the gusts of wind, John could hear him shrieking for breath.

"Right – I'm going to crawl out on to the plank and try to pull you up," Courtney shouted. "You understand what I'm saying? So don't panic – I'm coming to get you."

"Wait!" said John. "You're heavier than me, and you're stronger then me, too. I'll go out on the plank and you hold on to my ankles. Lucy, Uncle Robin – you can hold on to Courtney's waist."

Mr Cleat kept screaming and screaming. John climbed on to the plank and began to crawl along it on his hands and knees. It was difficult to balance on it because it was wet and slippery with mud and Mr Cleat was tugging at it so frantically.

He was only halfway along it when he felt it begin to tip forward.

"John!" shouted Uncle Robin. "Hurry up, John! The board's being pulled in too!"

212

Mr Cleat looked at John wild-eyed. He stopped screaming and held out one hand. "Save me," he said, so quietly that John could hardly hear him.

John reached forward and managed to touch Mr Cleat's fingertips. There was a split-second when he thought he might be able to get a grip on him. But then the board tipped even more and he almost fell off it. He put out his hand to stop himself from falling and momentarily touched the grass. It rippled as if it were a living beast and he snatched his hand away at once.

"John! You'll have to come back!" Courtney told him.

John stared at Mr Cleat and Mr Cleat stared back at him. John tried to edge forward a little further but Courtney was holding his ankles tight and wouldn't let him.

"*No!*" screamed Mr Cleat, as John crawled away from him, "*No!*" Courtney managed to pull John off the plank and safely away from the ley line.

They watched in helpless horror as Mr Cleat gripped the builder's board even more tightly and tried to pull himself up on to it. He was whimpering with determination and fear. He managed to shift one hand so that it was a little further up the board, but the forces that were dragging him into the ground were far too powerful. His elbows sank into the lawn, and then his shoulders, and as they did so the board tilted upward and was dragged in with him.

At the last, his lungs must have been too tightly compressed for him to speak. Nothing was showing but his head, and the plank which reared up in front of him at an angle of forty-five degrees. Looking sadly up at the sky, he was mute, and utterly beyond help. Then the grass swallowed him, and he was gone, leaving nothing behind him but the plank. That, too, was pulled into the ground, until only a metre and a half protruded from the lawn, like a headstone in a cemetery.

Lucy turned away and Uncle Robin put his arms around her. Uncle Robin himself was grim-faced. "Come on," he said. "It's time we went."

Another fork of lightning flickered out of the sky and went to earth on the other side of the street. There was a moment's hush, when all they could hear was the rain falling and the wind *shushing* in the trees. Then even the rain seemed to pause.

Seconds later, however, the whole garden was shaken with a high-explosive blast of thunder.

"Let's *go!*" shouted Courtney. "This plan of yours isn't going to work, John, and I just want to be out of here!"

What happened next, though, seemed almost miraculous. The instant the thunder died away, they heard the crackling of more lightning. They stopped and turned, and all had the same instinctive feeling about what was going to happen.

A second's silence. Then, out of the clouds, came a long, thin leader-stroke of lightning, searching hesitantly this way and that, a skeletal voodoo-arm made of pure electricity. It looked as if it were going to strike the weathervane on top of the house, but it suddenly jerked sideways and touched the top of the scaffolding pole in the garden.

Then the main bolt of lightning hit the pole and it was almost like the end of the world. Two hundred thousand volts, blinding all of them before tearing down the length of the pole and into the earth beneath. There was an ear-splitting crack of superheated air – hotter for one hundredth of a second than the surface of the sun.

The lightning must have scored a direct hit on the ley line, because a line of bright fire rushed off in both directions, north and south. Where it went north, it set fire to trees and bushes and blew up one garden fence after another. They could hear greenhouses exploding. They could hear walls collapsing. Where it went south, it scorched its way across the lawn and made the earth ripple and rumble like an earthquake. There was a terrible bursting noise, and Mr Cleat's body was flung right out of the ground and into the air, smoking and burned and hideously disjointed. The plank burst out, too, and was thrown blazing into the next door neighbours' garden.

The lightning tore towards the house but when it reached the outside walls it seemed to disappear.

They waited and waited and nothing happened. "Maybe that's it," said Courtney. "Maybe that's all it needed to do." Lucy took hold of John's hand. She was shivering with shock. She turned and caught sight of Mr Cleat's smoking body lying in the rain and quickly turned her face away. Although it was so dark, it was still possible to make out a horribly twisted grimace.

Courtney laid his hand on John's shoulder, and it was then that 66 Mountjoy Avenue blew up.

"*Get down!*" Courtney shouted, and the four of them dropped to the ground as the windows shattered and they were caught in a blizzard of broken glass. The entire roof was blasted up into the air – tiles and timbers scattered everywhere, and a huge ball of orange fire rolled up into the clouds. The chimney stacks collapsed, the side walls dropped outwards into the garden, the scaffolding fell, and the staircase tumbled sideways.

After that, the whole house burned with a grim ferocity, as if it were determined to consume itself before anybody else could have it. Tiles came crashing from the sky, burning curtains flew through the rain like vampires. The house crackled and spat as it burned itself up. Floors fell through, beds blazed, doors and walls were lost to the greedy flames.

"Mr Vane's still in there," said Lucy.

"So what are you going to do?" said Courtney. "Rush in and save him? After what he's done?"

John said, "We don't need to save him. He can live for ever."

"Not if his body's burned," Uncle Robin put in. "Even immortals can be destroyed by fire. Fire or impaling – that's what kills them. Why do you think they used to drive stakes into vampires' bodies and burn their coffins?"

"We have to go and look," said Lucy. "We can't just leave him to burn. That's murder."

"And what he did, that wasn't murder?"

"Of course it was. But that doesn't mean that we've got to behave as badly as him, does it? I mean, it's not up to us to try him and execute him, is it?"

"I don't think it's up to us to save him, either."

All the same, they made their way around to the front of the blazing house. It was only when they reached the front garden that they realized how devastating the damage was. 66 Mountjoy Avenue was nothing more than a few partially upright walls and a criss-cross collection of blazing timbers. Flames and sparks whirled up into the thundery sky, and the fire was so hot that the rain did nothing at all to damp it down.

Surprisingly, all that was left was the porch –

inviting you to walk in between the stone lions, up the steps, and open the front door right into hell.

"He can't be alive," said Lucy. "There isn't a hope."

They were still standing outside the house when neighbours and bystanders started to gather. The sky was beginning to clear, and in the distance the sun was shining on the wet rooftops of Tooting.

"I've called the emergency services," said an elderly man with a golf umbrella, and they could already hear the whooping of sirens in the distance.

"What happened?" asked a grey-haired woman in a spotted rain hat. "Was it gas?"

"Unexploded bomb, that's what I reckon it was," said a postman. "There was dozens of 'em round here, during the war."

Flames leaped up from the inside of 66 Mountjoy Avenue, nearly twenty metres high. A big woman in a hat came up to them and said, "Anybody hurt? I'm a first-aider."

John didn't know what to tell her. Mr Vane and Mr Cleat were both far beyond first-aid – as were all the hundreds of people who had bought houses from them over the years. First-aid? How can you give first-aid to a reliquary of human bones? No amount of bandages and liniment could ever heal what the Druid spirits had done.

John suddenly felt very tired.

The fire engines arrived, and the police, and the paramedics. John and the others were pushed to the sidelines while the flames were put out and the bodies taken away.

Courtney took hold of John's hand and grinned at him. "You did it, man. I didn't think you could. But you did it. I don't think anybody's going to be hearing from those Druids again, do you?"

19

Detective Inspector Carter said, "Cases like this, they get right up my nose."

John didn't know what to say. He had been answering Carter's questions for over half an hour now, and he had tried to be as truthful as possible. On the other hand, he hadn't told him anything about the Druids and the ley lines. He and the others had agreed not to. They knew that the police wouldn't believe them. And, more importantly, they still had to go round to each of Mr Vane's houses and close the gateway to the world beneath the ground.

The police might not believe in Druid spirits from the Iron Age, but once they realized that all of the houses were somehow connected, John and his friends wouldn't have a chance of getting into them and doing what they had to do.

Detective Inspector Carter swallowed a mouthful of cold coffee from a styrofoam cup, and pulled a face. "Cases like this, they start out simply baffling, you know what I mean? *Police are baffled by bricked-up bones mystery*. But instead of getting less baffling, they get even more baffling, until they're so baffling that you've forgotten what it is that you were baffled by."

John said, "I've told you everything that happened."

"I know you told me everything that happened. But what happened doesn't make any sense. I've got a blown-up house, I've got a dead man lying in the garden, and the more you explain it to me the less I understand it."

He pulled out a chair and sat down. "Let's go over this one more time. Mr Vane told you to meet him yesterday afternoon at 66 Mountjoy Avenue?"

"He said that he was going to be showing some clients around, and he wanted me to see how a professional did it."

"But when you got there, there were no clients, only him?"

"That's right, yes."

"And then your friends from the office arrived because they were worried about you?"

"That's right."

"Why were they so worried? They didn't have any reason to think that Mr Vane was going to hurt you, did they? Or did they?"

"They were just worried. Mr Rogers had disappeared when he went to see 66 Mountjoy Avenue and I suppose they didn't want anything like that to happen to me."

"So then what? You and your friends left the house, went out into the garden, and stuck a scaffolding pole in the flowerbed?"

"That's right."

"And you did that as a kind of makeshift lightning conductor?"

"We didn't want the house to be struck by lightning."

Inspector Carter blew out his cheeks in exasperation. "Your friends are saying the same thing. But this is where I lose you, John. What on earth made you think that the house was going to be struck by lightning? I mean, what are the odds on that? And why should you care so much anyway?"

"The house was on our books. We had a duty to protect it."

"Whenever there's a thunderstorm, do you go round to *all* of the houses on your books and stick scaffolding poles in the garden?"

"Well, no, we don't. It would take too long."

Carter covered his eyes with his hands. He was a man trying very, very hard to understand. "You didn't want the house to be struck by lightning, but as a consequence of your sticking a scaffolding pole in the flowerbed, your colleague Mr David Cleat was killed and the whole place was blown to smithereens."

"We didn't realize that would happen."

"No, well. Our scene-of-crimes officer can't work out how it happened, either. Normally, a lightning strike would have gone right into the ground, and caused nothing more than limited burns. In this case, however, it looks as if it travelled horizontally along a straight line, three or four miles north and three or four miles south. Apart from killing Mr Cleat and destroying 66 Mountjoy Avenue it caused about £150,000 worth of damage. Sheds, conservatories, that kind of thing."

"I know. We're sorry about that."

"Sorry? Yes, so am I. But I can't exactly charge you for sticking a scaffolding pole in the ground, can I?"

"I don't know. I don't know the law that well."

Inspector Carter gave him a sharp sideways look to make sure that he wasn't taking the mickey. Then he said, "What *I* can't work out is what happened to Mr Vane. His car was still outside, so he didn't drive away from the house. I can't see him *walking* away in a thunderstorm like that, can you? So far as we know, he wasn't in the house when it blew up. At least, we haven't yet found his remains."

At that moment there was a knock at the door and Sergeant Bynoe came in. "Have a word, guv?"

He bent over and murmured something in Carter's ear. John could see the Inspector's eyes widen.

Carter waited until Bynoe had left the room, and then he stood up and paced around the table. "We *have* discovered some remains, as it happens. The fire brigade were demolishing an unsafe wall at the back of the house when they came across a room full of human skeletons. Seventy or eighty people, by the looks of it. Completely bricked up, completely inaccessible. And yet at least one of the skeletons looks as if it's only a few days old."

He leaned over John and breathed peppermint breath-freshener all over him. "You wouldn't happen to know anything about *that*, would you?"

John shook his head violently.

Inspector Carter kept on staring at him for almost half a minute. Then he stood up straight and walked back around the table. "I hope you're not hiding something from me, John. Because if you are, you could be in a lot of trouble."

John said nothing. He could just imagine how Carter would react if he told him the truth. And besides, he was growing impatient to join Lucy and the others.

They had business to attend to.

He met them at The Feathers and they had cheese rolls and crisps for lunch. They were all looking tired and bruised, and they got a few funny looks from the other people in the pub.

Lucy said, "We've all had a pretty hard morning, so let's just start with a couple of houses, shall we? How about Abingdon Gardens and Greyhound Road? Abingdon Gardens first, that's the nearest. Then tomorrow we can work out a plan to go round the country and sort out all the rest of them."

She lifted the bunch of duplicate keys from her handbag. "One down and twenty-six to go."

Courtney said, "I've got a mallet and a pickaxe in the car. I just hope the police don't pick me up for going equipped."

They left the pub and drove in Courtney's BMW to Abingdon Gardens. After yesterday's storm the air was much clearer, and the sun was shining. John sat in the back of the car with Lucy and she reached over and held his hand.

"You realize that now Mr Vane's gone we're out of a job?" said Lucy.

"They haven't found his body yet."

"It probably burned to ashes. You saw how hot that fire was."

"Even if he *did* manage to get out, he certainly wouldn't keep us lot on, would he?"

"It's Cleaty I feel sorry for."

"Yes, but he knew what Mr Vane was doing and all he did was look the other way."

They reached the house at the end of Abingdon Gardens. As Lucy climbed out of the car she said, "This place still gives me the creeps."

Even though the sun was shining, the house looked damp and dingy and neglected. Its windows were like empty eyes. The three of them approached it with trepidation and climbed the front steps. Lucy was first and opened the door. Courtney followed her with his mallet and his pickaxe.

The house was chilly inside. They paused for a moment in the hallway and listened, but all they could hear was the persistent warbling of a pigeon sitting on one of the chimneys.

"Come on," said Lucy, and led the way into the living-room.

The fireplace here wasn't as large as 66 Mountjoy Avenue, and it was tiled in green mottled ceramic. All the same, it shared one essential feature – a rough-hewn block of stone about the size of a housebrick, in the centre just above the grate. There were five twig-shaped characters hewn on the stone – runes.

"Right," said John. "The sooner we get that stone out, the better."

Courtney took off his smart yellow coat, rolled up his sleeves, and lifted the pickaxe. "Stand clear, everybody. Man at work."

He hit the stone with his first blow, chipping some of it away. He hit it again, and this time he managed to crack the mortar which held it in place. He hit it a third time, and it dropped out of the fireplace and on to the floor.

"There, easy. Now all we have to do is smash it to bits."

"It's like Bath stone, it's pretty soft."

Courtney raised his mallet and gave the stone a blow which broke it in half. He was about to swing again when the door to the dining-room suddenly and silently swung open. Lucy jumped in shock, and Courtney lowered his mallet.

"Don't worry," said John, stepping across to close it. "It's only the wi—"

The door swung open wider and into the room limped Mr Vane. His eyes were wide and wild and the side of his face was caked with dark dried blood. Both of his hands were heavily bandaged with torn strips of sheet. He stood staring at them, saying nothing, his face engraved with bitterness and hatred.

"We thought you were dead," said Lucy, at last. "Do you need to see a doctor?"

Mr Vane limped into the middle of the room and looked down at the broken stone. Then he stared at each of them in turn. "Have you any idea what you've done?"

"I hope we've managed to stop you sacrificing any more people," said Lucy.

"People!" spat Mr Vane. "You don't know the half of what this world of ours is all about. You don't have any conception! You speak to me of *people*! I speak to you of *gods*! I speak to you of men with magic that could move the hills! I speak of their surviving spirits, who could one day rise up again and work their sorcery so that – *people* – like you would have to kneel down and worship them!"

"Whatever you think, you didn't have any right to *kill*," said John.

Mr Vane ignored him and slowly circled the room, his right foot dragging. "I managed to get out of the house before you sent that lightning-bolt along the ley line." His mouth worked in anguish and he was so furious that he could barely speak. "That lightning-bolt evaporated hundreds of Druid spirits. Some of the greatest names from our Druidic past. You could hear a scream running along the ley lines from one side of the country to the other. A whole magical heritage has been lost. A whole civilization. It was history itself that died yesterday."

Lucy said, "People are history, not ghosts."

Mr Vane touched the broken Druidic stone with his foot. "And now what are you planning to do?

Close *all* of the gateways between the real world and the magical world? What practical, pragmatic, *unimaginative* young creatures you are! You don't want anything dangerous in your lives, do you? You don't want anything which you can't explain."

He took a deep, quivering breath. "I've got news for you youngsters. You're not going to succeed. Those gateways are going to stay open. There are still some Druid spirits left; and when today's Druids die, their spirits will live on, too. I may have wearied of giving them sacrifices, and I may not have been able to persuade you to do it, John. But I will find somebody who will. There is always somebody who can be tempted by the idea of immortality. The Druids will still survive in this country long after you have been forgotten."

"I don't think so," said Courtney.

"You don't *think* so?"

"That's right. For the simple reason that we're going to stop you."

Mr Vane smiled at them, and then he actually laughed.

"What's so funny?" John challenged him.

"You are," said Mr Vane. "You really don't know just how much you amuse me with all of your misdirected bravado." He lifted his head and called out, "*Aedd! Aedd Mawr!*"

Behind them, they heard a soft dragging noise. The door was slammed back against the wall, and the statue walked in. But it didn't look like the statue they had first discovered. It was black and charred all over and part of one of its arms was missing, leaving a pointed stump. Its ivory face had been crudely nailed back into place, but it was badly burned on one side, so that it no longer looked calm and serene. It had a terrible injured snarl that made all of them step back apprehensively.

Mr Vane said, "I managed to drag him out of the flames. I burned both of my hands doing it. Look." He gripped one of the torn sheets in his teeth and unwrapped his left hand. It was nothing but a raw, blackened mitt, with no fingers at all. He waved it under Lucy's nose and Lucy recoiled in horror.

"I saved Aedd Mawr and I shall have my just reward for that, don't you worry! While *you* – you will get your just reward for what you have done."

Without warning, the statue reached out with its one good hand and seized Lucy by the arm. Courtney swung at it with his mallet, but the statue lashed out with its pointed stump and sent him flying back against the wall.

John tried to tug Lucy out of the statue's grip, but it was far too strong. It pulled her right up against its charred chest, with its forearm tight across her throat. Lucy gagged and kicked her legs.

Courtney got up again, and swung the mallet around and around. Mr Vane retreated behind the statue's back. "It's no good, you know. You can't hit either of us without hitting Lucy, and if you don't put the hammer down I shall ask my friend here to break her neck."

John said, "Leave her alone ... I'm warning you. Leave her alone."

He bent down and grabbed the pickaxe.

"And what are you going to do with that?" Mr Vane taunted him. "You're such a child you can hardly lift it."

Courtney tried to feint around the statue, but it shuffled to one side with its arm still around Lucy's throat, and Mr Vane still hovering right behind it.

John said, "It's no good, Courtney. We're going to have to give in."

"What? We've got rid of most of his spirit friends. How long do you think he can keep this up?"

"It's no good, Courtney. You've seen what he's like. He'll tell the statue to kill Lucy and we won't be able to stop him."

John stepped forward and stood only half a metre away from the statue. It stared back at him with its burned, twisted face.

"I don't know what kind of spirit lives inside you," he said, "but I'm asking you not to hurt this girl, and to let her go."

"I want your solemn promise not to damage any more runestones," said Mr Vane.

John nodded, and said, "All right. I promise. We all promise."

"Good," smiled Mr Vane. "And to make sure you keep it, I'm going to ask Aedd Mawr to strangle young Lucy right in front of your eyes. No Druid promise can ever be binding without a sacrifice."

"*No!*" John shouted, and tried again to pull at Lucy's arm, but the statue waved his pointed stump at her and squeezed Lucy's throat so tightly that she let out a high, cackling gargle. John was frightened, but he was frustrated and enraged too. "You promised to set her free!"

"And so I shall. Free from her mortal body. Free to roam along the ley lines with the other spirits."

"You even *bruise* her, I'll break every bone in your body!" Courtney yelled.

Mr Vane threw back his head and laughed even louder. "After all these years, after all these hundreds of sacrifices, what do you think one more life means to me?"

John hesitated for a moment. But then the statue grasped Lucy's throat even more tightly, and she began to turn pink. John ducked his head down and rolled forward on the floor, in the same way that he'd seen cops on American TV shows do. He ended up right behind Mr Vane, back on his feet again, the pickaxe clutched in both hands.

It seemed to happen in slow motion. John had never imagined that he would be able to do anything like this and he wasn't sure that he could do it even now. He saw Mr Vane turning his head, his yellow teeth bared in surprise. He heard Lucy choking again. He lifted the pickaxe sideways and swung it behind his head.

"*Nooo!*" cried Mr Vane. But John whacked the point of the pickaxe right into his back. It pierced his chest and drove deep into the statue. *Crunch – thud*. Mr Vane said nothing more than "*Uggh!*" and tried to reach behind him with one bandaged hand to pull the pickaxe out of his back.

But the statue threw back its arms and let out a roar of pain and fury that sounded like a thousand voices all roaring at once. Courtney snatched Lucy well away from it as it staggered around the living-room with Mr Vane pinned to its back, his feet scrabbling helplessly on the floor.

The statue gave one last bellow and then he and Mr Vane toppled sideways with a deafening crash.

Mr Vane lay with one hand resting on the statue's charred shoulder. A thin stream of blood ran from the side of his mouth.

Courtney knelt beside him and said, "Hold still – I'm going to try to get the pickaxe out."

"No, no ... don't do that. It's too late now, and I don't want any more pain." He looked up at them with dimming eyes. "I'm glad it's over," he whispered.

Lucy turned away and John held her very tight. Courtney got to his feet and said, "Blowing up the house was bad enough. How are we going to explain this one?"

But even as they watched, it looked as if the statue were beginning to sink into the floor, and Mr Vane with it. Gradually its pointed stump disappeared, and then its shoulder. Within a few minutes there was nothing left of either of them except two arms, one wooden and one human, lying side by side on the floorboards.

Then, without a sound, they were gone.

John said, "We broke the stone. How come they could still be sucked into the floor?"

"Ah – look. We broke it in half, but the lettering's still intact. That's a lesson we need to learn when we go around and get rid of all the rest of them."

"Right now," said Lucy, "all I want to do is to go home."

They finished the job two weeks later, knocking the Druidic runestone from a large family house overlooking the Derbyshire Dales. Courtney gave it to Lucy and said, "Make sure you break it up as small as you can." Lucy took it out into the garden while John and Courtney took a last look around the house.

"Well, I'm glad this is all over," said John, unconsciously echoing Mr Vane's last words.

Courtney clapped him on the back and said, "Come on, let's get out of here. I could do with some lunch."

It was a warm, breezy afternoon as they closed the garden gate behind them and walked back to Courtney's car. Lucy was already waiting for them.

"Well, what are we going to do now?" asked Courtney. "Now that we've stopped being saviours of the world as we know it, all we are is three out-of-work estate agents."

"Perhaps we should start our own agency," Lucy suggested. "The three of us could get together and rent an office, surely?"

"I can see it now," said Courtney. "Tulloch, Mears and French. The slickest estate agents ever. Glossy colour brochures, weekly ads in *Country Life*..."

"No," said John. "I've got a better idea. 'Gaffs' ... the estate agents who tell you exactly what's wrong with a house before they sell it to you. Noisy neighbours? Subsidence? Dry rot? We don't hide anything."

"What about skeletons in the wall?" said Lucy.

A large cloud passed over the sun and suddenly the afternoon seemed chilly. They climbed into the car and they were well on their way home again before it began to brighten up.

The following afternoon, Lucy went round to see Uncle Robin. He was out in the garden, shaking nuts and raisins on to his birdtable. A little red-and-green windmill whirred in the afternoon wind.

"Did you get it for me?" Uncle Robin asked her.

She handed him the padded postal bag, and he hefted it in his hand to feel its weight. "Well done, Lucy. You're a very good girl. You always were.

"Do you know something?" he said, turning away from the birdtable. "The Druids were cruel, and merciless, but they were the greatest magicians that this country has ever known, or ever *will* know."

Once inside the kitchen, he reached inside the bag and took out the stone, with its runic inscriptions. He turned it this way and that, examining it from all sides, and finally put it down.

"It won't cause any trouble, will it?" asked Lucy. "You only need it for research. I mean, there won't be any more sacrifices, or anything like that, will there?"

"Of course not," said Uncle Robin, his eyes bright with anticipation. "But now I can study the Druidic spirits directly ... at first hand. Now I have a way to *communicate* with them. This is like finding a way to talk to the Ancient Greeks, or the lost people of Atlantis. It would have been a disaster to lose such a civilization completely."

"I have to go now," Lucy told him. "I'm meeting John this evening. He's taking me to a club."

"Nice chap, John," said Uncle Robin. "But you won't tell him about *this*, will you?"

Lucy shook her head.

"Good," Uncle Robin said. "This can be our little secret..."